# LETHAL ASSAULT

## THE JUSTICE TRILOGY BOOK TWO

STEPHEN MERTZ

ROUGH
EDGES
PRESS

# PRAISE FOR STEPHEN MERTZ

*"A Grandmaster of action/adventure novels!*
    —MensAdventureMagazines&Books.com

*"One of the best adventure writers of our time!"*
    —James M. Reasoner

*"Stephen Mertz writes a hard-edged, fast-paced thriller for those who like their tales straight and sharp!"*
    —Joe R. Lansdale

*"The cleanest, strongest prose in the business!"*
    —Gravetapping.com

*"The Mertz Formula: rousing action and an exciting plot!"*
    —Prof. Wm. H. Young, A Study of Adventure Fiction

*"One of the best writers in the genre!"*
    —Max Allan Collins

**Lethal Assault**
Paperback Edition
© Copyright 2022 Stephen Mertz

Rough Edges Press
An Imprint of Wolfpack Publishing
5130 S. Fort Apache Rd. 215-380
Las Vegas, NV 89148

roughedgespress.com

Paperback ISBN 978-1-68549-068-3
LCCN 2022935616

# LETHAL ASSAULT

# CHAPTER ONE

*Moscow*, thought Jack Cody, *is beautiful at night.*

Of course, it all depended on your vantage. Twisting in his harness 1,000 feet above the sidewalks of Krasnoskaya Prospect at 2 in the morning gave Cody a unique view. He felt the dry, bitter cold, heard the rope flex and his equipment clank. He marveled at the jeweled chaos of a thousand lit windows and neon signs glittering far below. Modern Moscow was more than just a historic wonder: it was a hub of commerce and industry, as well as one of the most popular cities in the world for tourists. That a metropolitan area of 12 million people could be hushed to cathedral silence simply amazed him. Any other city would still be noisy at this hour. But here in the heart of the Russian Federation – Putin's Russia – cities, like their residents, tended to behave themselves.

Working quickly, he double-checked the clamps for both his main and safety lines, eye following the ropes to the rooftop's edge. There on the roof of the Vostok Tower of the Federation skyscraper complex was his anchor point, an air conditioning housing. Parked close by was the 'borrowed' all-black military-grade Epsilon microlight he had piloted here, keeping below air control radar.

The Epsilon was next generation, "bleeding-edge" aviation technology. Emerging from the sorcerous caverns of Lockheed's "skunkworks", the Epsilon maintained the basic microlight design of a motorized glider but came equipped with some fancy extras. Special anechoic fabric had been used to stitch the cloth frame together around the lightweight black struts, making the bird stealth capable. A phalanx of nearly weightless surface-to-ground "needle" missiles was affixed to the fuselage, each one capable of taking out an armored vehicle. The Epsilon could fly, fight and hide from just about any AWAC or radar system known to man. And, in flight, it made a sound barely louder than your average lawn mower. It was the perfect craft for a mission like this, and Cody felt lucky to have one available.

The tower's curved roof had made landing tricky, even with the Epsilon's magnetic clamp gear and VTOL capability. But now it was safely anchored to the roof. The plan was to detonate the unit once he had gained entry through the plate-glass windows, leaving behind only charred wreckage to be wondered at by tomorrow's maintenance crews. But until that happened, the microlight was his Plan B for escape in case the infiltration didn't go as planned.

A gust of wind punched him and Cody had to tack back to regain his line of descent. He released his top and then bottom grip-winch, lowering himself foot by foot past floors sheathed in plate glass. Most were dark, but the odd lit floors were uninhabited save for one. A janitor stood, back turned, hunched over her cellphone as he glided by noiselessly.

*Some things*, he reflected, *never change, regardless of the city.*

Keeping count of the floors, he continued lowering himself. Two levels below the 89th floor observation deck were the offices of Egor Krupin, well-heeled billionaire and Who's-Who member of the Moscow business elite. To the stock markets of the world, Krupin was the friendly, bearded face of Russian billionaire philanthropy. But to Cody and his controllers in CIA, he was a target of interest.

INTERPOL's rap-sheet on Krupin was a mile long. Krupin Investments, a financial umbrella corporation with controlling interest in a hundred companies, was known to act as a money-laundering hub for the Russian *mefiya*. Krupin himself was a ranking Bretva boss, a rumored human trafficker whose connections extended deep into the netherworld where illegal Russian arms sales intersected with criminals and terrorists. Krupin had surfaced on both FBI's and INTERPOL's radar for illegal activity. But he had only recently come to the attention o American intelligence.

Krupin was connected to General Vetrov, the man responsible for the disappearance and re-sale of Russian nuclear weapons. Once attached to the Russian general staff, Vetrov had recently "disappeared" so far as legitimate governments and intelligence services were aware. But far from vanishing, the man had thrown in with an American – Thelma Justice, international celebrity and women's empowerment guru. Where Vetrov's crimes centered around trafficking nukes, Thelma Justice also had blood on her hands. Her organization, the Order of World Harmony, had recently demonstrated its willingness to kill to obtain Biblical antiquities – specifically, a relic in possession of Cody's team. Krupin was one point of connection between Vetrov and Thelma Justice.

He planned to pay Krupin's offices a visit.

A noise intruded – a distant clicking that resolved into the clippity-clop of horses' hooves. Cody looked down and saw the ant-sized figures of Russian police on horseback passing through the high-rise canyon far below. Moscow Police Service possessed the largest cavalry force in Europe, with officers of their First Operational Regiment routinely patrolling the city on horseback. Fortunately, their attention remained at street level. Code watched them until they vanished into shadows at the far end, then continued his descent.

Climbing is not a skillset trained into American intelligence or special forces personnel. Cody had learned during a slow and painful two-week immersion in a classified NATO advanced mountain warfare course called X-ASCENT. Cody, one of the American contingent that included two Green Berets and a Navy SEAL, had been the last American standing after attrition by injury. The core group of youthful Canadian and Norwegian spec warriors, all rated climbers, had been dismissive of their greenhorn American colleagues. Cody alone had earned their grudging admiration, being christened into their fraternity with the nickname 'Old Man' and traditional schnapps toast upon completion of their graduation climb up Aconcagua. He was one of three master climbers in the US special forces arsenal.

He lowered himself to the 87th floor, which was owned entirely by Krupin. Working quickly, he selected a window and set a golf ball-sized chunk of thermal plastique at each corner and one dead center. The plan was to detonate, implode the glass and gain entry.

For one brief moment, Cody was transported back in time to another explosion – one every bit as precise and as carefully planned as the one he now prepared. That detonation – a car bomb, meant for him – had ended the lives of his wife Carol and his children. Their absence, and the howling void within that drove him on, was never far from him in moments like this, on missions which, per Agency agreement, he only took on if there was little or no chance of success.

"Suicide" Cody, they called him. And right now, he was coming for Krupin.

Once he had done what he had come to do, he would take the elevator down to the lobby and rendezvous with his ground team, waiting in a surveillance van on the street below. Drawing the remote detonator from a pocket of his windbreaker, he glanced down and wondered how they were doing.

# CHAPTER TWO

KRASNOSKAYA PROSPECT WAS DESERTED. Two
Moscow city police officers were able to guide their
horses side-by-side up the middle of the street. They
chatted quietly together, filling the graveyard shift with
gossip and off-color jokes. Very little happened in this
section of the city after hours. Which was why, noting an
anomaly, they slowed by the lobby of the Vostok Tower.

Urban Russians tended not to be a nocturnal lot.
Weekend evenings or settings where young people gathered were an exception, but for the most part the streets
tended to be quiet after dark. Which was why this
anomaly stood out. Someone had parked and left a van
by the curb.

The mounted officers split up, one inspecting the
roof and side panels while the other circled around to
peer through the windshield. The van's presence was not
a traffic violation per se, but it was unusual enough at
this hour to merit a quick once-over. The horseman at
the front bent and squinted at the dark glass, then
straightened when his partner whistled.

The cop at the rear of the van was shining his flashlight at the side panel. The one in front joined his partner, recognizing the red, blue and white logo of Rostelecom, Russia's largest cable TV and internet service provider. Such vans were common sights in all areas of the country. That one might be left parked overnight during a multi-day installation was not impossible (or even terribly unusual). And so this anomaly was proving to be of the rather dull kind – not the sort of thing for busy cops to waste their time on.

The two policemen exchanged a shrug. The one with a flashlight smirked. *"Pornografiya,"* he joked and his partner chuckled. Dousing the flashlight, they made a quick radio report by walkie-talkie before the two returned to their patrol, clopping off down the street.

Inside the dark, stuffy interior of the van, CIA officer Sara Durrell breathed a sigh of relief.

She was a good-looking, athletic woman in her thirties. With a toned body and an instinctive understanding of her own charms, she was a formidable presence in the Agency's middle ranks. Until crossing paths with Parnell, the officious little man responsible for her suspension from duty. It was her old friend Jack Cody – friend turned partner, now lover – who had brought her from her bureaucratic purgatory into a new role.

To say that her and Cody's circumstances were precarious was an understatement of thermonuclear proportions. As far as CIA was concerned, Sara Durrell had done the unthinkable for a senior officer. Company procedures demanded that agents with security clearance remain in constant touch with Langley, their location known to DCI staff at all times. But Sara had discarded her microchipped ID badge in a trashcan and swapped her Company-issued Blackberry for a burner phone. She and Cody were in the wind, off the radar and in big trouble. And it all had to do with the slender, quiet young woman with her in the surveillance van.

The young woman's name was Princess Aisha bint al-Ahmad. Sara had wandered oh-so-slightly off the CIA reservation by tracking Aisha down via unconventional means. Which is to say, rather than informing her control officer, submitting a mission brief and assembling a team, she had simply gone off and done it on her own. Her reasons had been compelling enough: Aisha was said to have information regarding a missing archaeological relic of geopolitical significance. And this had proven true. The fragment was significant enough to attract the attention from many, including those who had intercepted and knocked Sara unconscious as she attempted to make contact with Aisha at a Thelma Justice rally in DC.

Sara had paid the price for her insubordination. Relieved of duty, placed on administrative leave and nominally under investigation, she had been under the worst of bureaucratic clouds when events took a turn, forcing her back into action. Aisha, intercepted by her brother for a forced return home to the Emirates, had been rescued by Cody at Sara's behest. Now the three of them were on the run.

*And not just from CIA,* thought Sara, examining Aisha in the half-light of the van's rear. The young Emirati noblewoman was important enough to attract notice from many quarters, including the Vatican itself.

"How are you doing?" Sara asked quietly.

"I am fine." Aisha shifted slightly in her padded chair and examined the display monitors on the van's surveillance array. "You heard the radio transmission?"

"The squawk?" Sara nodded. "What about it?"

"Our presence has been reported. The Russian police will follow up."

"Probably so." Sara checked her watch. "But our presence here is just an irregularity, nothing more. We should be long gone by the time a patrol car rolls up."

"Let us hope so," said Aisha. "My family is not popular with the Russian government."

*I bet,* thought Sara. Sheikh Reza al-Ahmad, Aisha's father, was a bitter critic of Russia's Middle East adventures. The sheikh was known to call in personal favors and spread his own *baksheesh* liberally to frustrate Moscow's initiatives in the region. Putting his daughter on ice in a Moscow police station would prove the diplomatic embarrassment of the decade for the honorable sheikh, now lying on his deathbed.

"I have not properly expressed my gratitude," Aisha said quietly. "You and your friend Mr. Cody are extremely brave and honorable. The House of al-Ahmad is indebted to you."

"You're welcome." In amidst the steely cool of her operational self, Sara felt an ember of real warmth kindling for the girl. Aisha was about as different from Sara as anyone could be. But despite the girl's privileged background and wonky attachment to feminist mega-guru Thelma Justice, she was proving to be more of a dark horse – and more self-sufficient – than Sara had expected. And she appreciated that.

*"Alpine to Base Camp ... Alpine to Base Camp ..."*

Cody's voice crackled across the secure radio link. Sara hit the transmit switch on the van's communication console. "Base Camp receiving you, Alpine."

*"Am about to blow the glass and head in. We're minutes out from exfil,"* he said.

"Roger that," said Sara. "We're five-by-five, here."

High above, she knew, Cody was preparing to detonate a window to enter the tower and toss the offices of Egor Krupin, a known confederate of General Vetrov. Both men had connections to the relic Aisha carried, and sufficient interest in its recovery to commit murder. Establishing the nature of that link was central to Cody's mission. Which seemed to be going by the numbers.

Until a knock came on the van's panel door.

# CHAPTER THREE

THE PRINCESS AISHA bint al-Ahmad felt her heart speed up in response to the knock. She tightened her gulp on the arms of her swivel chair, planted her feet and looked down at the floor of the van. She told herself to take long, even breaths. Reminded herself that to remain calm could mean the difference between life and death. So had it been since she had fled the Emirate just a few days ago.

Her decision barely made sense to anyone, herself included. Back home in her father's house, she was not only loved but also treated like royalty. For so she was. She had her own wing of the palace apartments and an entire retinue of servants to staff it. Her slightest whim could be answered by her merely breathing it aloud. But it was not enough.

Aisha bint al-Ahmad was many things: princess, sportswoman, eligible for marriage. But the one thing she was above all was curious. Her restless intellect had caused her to assemble around her not the eligible young bachelors or showbiz celebrities of her father's kingdom, but instead a small but dedicated group of university professors. In the local press, she was feted as a society persona. But to those who knew her, she was the Scholar Princess. Her area of interest was religious anthropology.

Another knock. Her eyes flashed to the door.

It was her doing that had brought them all here, her and her new friends.

At least, she *hoped* they were friends ...

Her studies had caused her to come into possession of something ancient – a clay tablet dating from early in the First Century. Since then, she had been on the run from everybody. Admiring female empowerment guru Thelma Justice, and hungry for answers, she had come to North America, hotly pursued by her brother Achmed and a team of Vatican operatives. A fateful clash between both parties had caused her to flee under the protection of Sara and Cody. That protection had brought her here, to Moscow. To this van parked by the Vostok Tower in the middle of the night.

And someone was knocking on the door.

# CHAPTER FOUR

CODY POSITIONED himself above and slightly to one side of the plate glass window then detonated the plastique.

The explosives made a popping sound no louder than a cough. The plate glass seemed to tense and freeze a moment before a tesserae of hair-thin cracks appeared. Then the glass crashed inwards, obeying the laws of shape charges and physics. Explosions, he knew, were like water: always seeking the path of least resistance. In this case that meant inward. The glass splintering made more sound than the explosion itself. The shards landed with muffled thumps on the carpeted floor inside.

Cody swung down and in.

He had lucked out. This window led into a roomy, private office. The door was, thankfully, closed. He stepped across the shag carpet littered with slivers of glass and put his hand on the doorknob. Before twisting it, he glanced back. There, beyond the shattered maw of broken plate glass, the twin black lines of his ropes drifted between he and the Moscow city lights. A fitful breeze blew, ruffling papers on the desk.

Cody pulled the door an inch from its jamb and peered out. A dark empty hallway stretched into shadow. He saw a glow of light at the far end and heard voices.

He pulled the side-arm he had drawn for this mission. Like the climbing gear, the microlight on the roof above and van on the street below, it was borrowed. Although not his weapon of first choice, a 9mm Browning would serve his needs adequately.

*Leave it to Parsons to equip me with a British gun,* he thought wryly. And edged out into the corridor.

# CHAPTER FIVE

THE KNOCK CAME AGAIN on the van door. Sara spun to the monitors. The camera hidden in the passenger side mirror was perfectly aligned to capture the knocker's image.

It was a Moscow city policeman, a beat cop working the neighborhood by foot. Sara recalled the radio squawk from the mounted patrolmen. *He's following up,* she thought. And now he was speaking. Bending her head, she closed her eyes and recalled her rudimentary Russian.

*Know ... in there ... saw van moving ...*

*Come out now.*

Sara checked the clock. Cody would be inside, tossing Krupin's office for another five minutes. All she had to do was buy a little time – delay just long enough for him to finish and come out. She scanned the van's interior, eventually settling on the black backpack Parsons had included with the equipment and weapons. Aisha's eyes followed Sara as she yanked open its zipper and produced a bottle of Bushmills Irish whiskey.

*What's this?* she'd asked Parsons.

*A sentimental gift. Your dear old uncle would never forgive me if I didn't continue the tradition with the next generation ...*

*Thank God for tradition*, Sara thought, unscrewing the cap and dabbing a little behind each ear. She upended the bottle, taking a swig and rinsing her mouth with the powerful whiskey before spitting it out into a coffee cup.

"Stay quiet," she ordered Alisha as she removed her suit jacket and unbuttoned her blouse to expose cleavage. Then she moved to the panel door.

Patrol Officer Pavel Ludmenko of the Moscow City Police wasn't sure what to expect when the panel door slid open. Most vehicles that met the criteria for "abandoned after hours" were unoccupied, but he knew this one wasn't. Careful observation combined with his years of experience confirmed the presence of passengers. Ludmenko noted the Rostelecom logo and ventured a guess that some homeless person had managed to break in to sleep off a drunk. So he was surprised when the door opened and a fit, attractive woman in her thirties emerged, a bottle of alcohol in hand.

Ludmenko grinned. "Hello, sweetheart," he said kindly. He dug in a pocket for his pen and ticket book. "You know you can't sleep in a van parked on the street, correct? So tell me what this is all about."

The woman took a swig of the bottle and struggled with a few words in Russian. He recognized the word 'damn' when she paused to mutter to herself.

"It's okay, sweetheart," he said, holding up a hand. "Is okay. Don't be afraid. I speak English. What is going on here?"

"Oh, thank God!" The woman laughed loudly. "My Russian sucks. My producer gave me a phrasebook but it's in my luggage somewhere." She gestured vaguely in the direction of uptown. "Ah! What can I say? We finished filming on the top floor and I got a little friendly with one of the camera operators. We decided to start the party down here in her van ..."

*Her*. Ludmenko nodded. To each his (or her) own. He wasn't one to judge.

"... and I s'pose we got carried away and, yeah. Now we're in trouble." She laughed and extended the bottle. "Sure ya' don't want a snort?"

"*Nyet*, no thank you." Ludmenko's head was down, his attention on his ticket book as he wrote. Public drunkenness, sleeping rough, parking infraction... He got it all down but added the notation that this was a foreigner. A slap on the wrist and a letter to her embassy would be the likely result. Arrest and jail was too extreme for such a mild offense. "You have passport, please?"

"Passport? Sure thing, cutey." Sara burped and turned back, unhitching the panel door that she had been careful to shut behind her. As it rolled open, she became simultaneously aware that Aisha was gone (most likely by stealth through the open driver's side door) and that the policeman was suddenly gasping.

Sara turned back in time to see Patrol Officer Pavel Ludmenko hit the ground, unconscious. Standing over him was Aisha, unarmed, apparently having just immobilized and KO'd him with her bare hands in two seconds flat.

"You told me to be quiet, not to stay in the van," she protested to Sara's look of annoyance.

*She's a dark horse, alright*, thought Sara.

"Okay. C'mon," Sara said, grasping the cop by the lapels and lifting. "Let's get him off the street before anyone sees us."

# CHAPTER SIX

THE GIRL from Volgograd was having a hard time staying awake. She remembered very little of the past nine hours, which was unusual for her because her mind was normally quite sharp. It had been sharp enough to carry her from technical college in her southwest industrial town here to Moscow, center of the Federation's power.

Many people in her town were unemployed, and a great many her age were unable to find work, even in large towns like Moscow. She had spent her first week here in a cold water flat with five other girls, furiously checking the want ads and eating take-out dinners. Three of the five had ended their search and returned home. She and a girl from Minsk had stayed and found work.

The girl had been thrilled to obtain a job in the general secretarial pool of the Vostok Towers office complex and overjoyed when her hard work had brought her to the attention of Mr. Krupin himself. All the secretaries knew who he was. One sight of the bald, bearded oligarch was enough to bring a hush over a roomful of employees. Krupin was a charismatic man – deep-voiced, confident and in possession of that quality which made everyone who came into his presence feel special. Blessed.

So, on the day he stopped by her desk and invited her to take a position in his offices on the 87th floor, she had accepted gladly. The looks of jealousy fired her way from the other office girls were legion, but the girl from Volgograd didn't care. She had packed up and re-established herself in a cubicle outside Mr. Krupin's office.

At first, the work had mostly been general secretarial stuff – sending e-mails, booking dates on the electronic calendar, answering phones. But as time went by, she took on more complex projects, some for Mr. Krupin himself.

The girl stumbled, losing a shoe. She was ... walking down a hallway? Apparently. And the pressure on her biceps. Oh, right! She was being helped along. By two of Mr. Krupin's "gentlemen."

Earlier that night, she had worked late finishing up a business plan the boss had assigned her to complete. To her surprise, Mr. Krupin was waiting in his office when she went to put it on his desk. The boss had taken a look, complimented her on her work and invited her to drink a toast with him. Together, they had raised glasses to the new venture being planned. At that moment, everything in her world had seemed right.

*Mr. Krupin is so kind,* she remembered thinking. And handsome. To work for such a man was surely a stroke of the most favorable fortune. A bright future lay ahead of her.

She had just taken the one drink but, shortly after, began to feel funny. Her legs went wobbly. Then these two gentleman had appeared – the same ones now walking her into a large, bare room festooned with lights and what appeared to be some kind of movie set.

*Where am I?*

Everything was fuzzy. *Who were these men?* She felt their hands on her jacket, her shirt as they undressed her. In some dim part of her mind, she knew she should resist but didn't. She was made to sit and another drink was offered — wine, this time. It was only when she looked down and saw her bare legs that she realized she was naked. Looking up, she saw Mr. Krupin standing a short distance away, his contours weaving slightly as he watched, a grin on his face as he oversaw this nightmare.

Lights. Camera. Were they filming?

And then she saw the razor. But was too far gone to scream.

# CHAPTER SEVEN

THE VOICES GOT LOUDER, and the light brightened as Cody approached the end of the corridor. This seemed like it would be a busy place during the day: the floor was crowded with cubicles and work rooms. Darkened offices lined either side of the hallway; he ducked into the one next to the lit room and listened. He heard the sounds of equipment and people shifting around, and a mix of Russian and English voices. He guessed perhaps a half-dozen people, perhaps as many as ten, were working on something in there. Cody held his breath and eased out into the hallway. Most peeping toms made the mistake of observing at eye level. An amateur's mistake. Going to one knee, he took a careful peek around the jamb into the open room.

Inside was a high-ceilinged, wide-open workspace. Carpeted in the same plush shag as the office he'd entered, the white walls on either side boasted wide, tall paint canvases – all the modernist work of the same artist so far as Cody could tell, and likely worth a mint. The back wall rose to a split-level balcony that overlooked the lower level. It had the feeling of a conference room with the tables and chairs removed. Instead of office furniture, the room was crowded with tall Klieg lights ringed with white baffles to focus the glare.

A three-man camera crew was positioning a tripod supporting an expensive digital movie camera. A handful of broad-shouldered toughs, dressed in turtlenecks and blazers appropriate to the setting but still sporting the tattoos and bling of street enforcers, loafed by the walls in attitudes of insouciant indifference. But their bravura only went so far. Because they were, after all, red-blooded young Russians, their eyes drifted now and then to the naked woman who was the focus of all the lights, camera and action.

*Drugged*, Cody decided. That accounted for her dazed, distracted manner, for her casual nakedness and total lack of self-consciousness in a room full of guys. Lolling on a couch draped in a white sheet, she was a vision – a gorgeous, slim-hipped red-head with perfectly-shaped breasts and a taut belly tapering to hard thighs that enclosed the furred cleft between. She reclined on her side, a wineglass in her hand from which she occasionally sipped. Whenever her arm tired, she set it down unsteadily on the small table beside her.

The last person in the room was Krupin.

Bald, broad-shouldered, the Russian executive more closely resembled a professional wrestler than anyone's idea of a prosperous businessman. He had his back turned to the door, arms crossed as he supervised the camera crew. The man wore an expensive blazer, chinos and high-end loafers. Cody caught a glimpse of the gold Rolex as Krupin unfolded and waved his arms for attention.

"Okay, okay! *Vnimaniye!* Listen!" He clapped his

hands. "Sweetheart! You ready for your close-up? We go now. Misha and Alexei come to you. They take you together, like we discussed, yes?"

The woman on the couch drained her wineglass, set it on the table with a click and shot Krupin a wobbly thumbs-up. Two of the five toughs standing around the walls began to strip. Cody wondered if Krupin's bodyguards received union rates for work as extras in his porno films...

He didn't notice the straight razor in the hand of the tall, thin enforcer until that same man stepped forward and pulled on a Halloween mask. Right then Cody noticed, too, that the man was dressed in Eighteenth Century garb - top hat, cape and dark suit. With the mask, he struck a Phantom of the Opera note. And with the razor, a little Sweeney Todd.

Krupin was gesturing now, communicating with the masked man over the flexing, moaning backs of the performers, drawing a finger across his throat in a cutting motion. That's when it hit him ...

*They're making a snuff film.*

A job like Cody's met with many moral forks-in-the-road. There had been times he had witnessed crimes being committed but by operational necessity been unable to intervene. Circumstances had forced him to abandon good people in tight spots because he was ordered to do so. And he had made God knows how many questionable judgments of his own. But one thing was clear. He was a US special forces soldier attached to the White House and he was going to be damned if he would just stand there and allow some innocent woman to be murdered right in front of his eyes.

The trio on the couch was approaching the climax (so to speak) of their scene. The man in the mask with the razor was stealing up behind them now. Krupin was bent over the camera crew, watching the action through the viewfinder. Now the girl on the couch began her big moment, working up from a series of whimpers to loud, declaratory screams. The man in the mask stood behind her and raised the razor.

That's when Cody stepped in, raised the Browning and a put a bullet through the center of his forehead.

The masked man folded, razor dropping from his hand. The woman gasped and stared, the men, too. Krupin whirled and dug at his beltline for the pistol holstered there. Cody fired and sent him scuttling for cover behind a stack of lighting equipment.

Meanwhile, the two naked toughs and the one left standing were reacting. The one by the wall pulled a chain from his pocket and began swinging. In an unexpected move, he let fly the thing, sending ten pounds of metal hurtling in Cody's direction. The chain tangled and wound around his gun-arm.

Krupin stepped from behind the equipment and fired. Now it was Cody's turn to seek cover. He rolled behind a stack of equipment cases and began shaking the chain from his gun hand. The nearest naked guy picked up a chair from the movie set and advanced, raising it over his head.

Krupin fired again. Cody pulled the last of the chain loose, raised his gun and shot the naked guy with the chair in the chest. The second naked guy took the hint and dove behind the couch for cover just as the girl suddenly seemed to sober up. She screamed, ran past the chain-slinger and took refuge beside Cody behind the cases.

*"Pomogi mne!"* she shrieked.

"All good!" He wrapped an arm around her, pushing

her down and scanning the room. Where was the camera crew? They appeared to have fled the moment the party started.

The naked guy rose from behind the couch with a machine pistol. God knows where he found it, but he opened fire with the damn thing anyway. The weapon made an unbelievable racket in the enclosed space. Bullets shredded the equipment cases, narrowly missing Cody. He was squeezing the woman close to him when he felt her stiffen, then suddenly slump.

*God, no!*

He checked. She'd taken a bullet.

The machine-pistol chattered again, joined this time by Krupin's gun. And now the third guy, chain man, was digging for something in an athletic bag.

A deep, volcanic rage seized Cody. The woman's death had been enough to ignite it. But it was not only for her. It was for the deaths of her and many other women. Carol's especially.

There was no place in that wilderness for mercy.

Cody shot the nearest man in the back of the head, then turned to the guy with the machine-pistol. Naked, a snarl on his face and flushed bright red from exertion, he was still firing, pockets of fat jiggling on his belly and sides with each salvo, bullets shredding the equipment cases. Cody crouched there by the ever-widening pool of blood seeping from the girl's body until ...

*Enough!*

He waited for a pause between bursts, leapt up and aimed the Browning. The naked guy's attention was down on his machine-pistol, fingers fumbling with the mechanism ...

Krupin emerged from behind cover and raised his gun ...

Cody raised his own and Krupin ducked back behind cover. Then he flicked the gun back and shot the second naked guy. A bullet hole appeared in his midriff and he crumpled, collapsing onto a glass table that exploded in a million shards. Krupin seized that opportunity to bolt through the door and escape.

*Five down*, thought Cody, reloading. *Time to finish the job.*

With one last look at the dead girl, he set off after Krupin.

# CHAPTER EIGHT

CODY HEARD the fire door slam at the far end of the corridor. He sprinted, clearing the distance in mere seconds and shouldering the door open to emerge onto a concrete landing. Lit by an emergency sign, two sets of stairs converged on the dim space, one up, one down. He paused and heard Krupin's footfalls clatter in the stairwell, heading down. He descended two at a time, pausing at each landing just long enough to ensure Krupin was still on the move.

Then, two landings down, he paused and heard nothing. Silence.

A fire door slammed two floors below him.

Krupin had taken refuge on the 83rd floor. Cody went after him.

Reaching the landing, he eased open the fire door and listened. Under the dim light, his sense of hearing was magnified. He heard footsteps and ragged breathing disappear into a room just down the hallway. Cody moved further onto the dark floor and paused to orient himself.

There! More noise. It sounded like Krupin moving something - a chair, probably - out of his way. *Panicked*, Cody realized. Krupin likely had no idea that Cody knew where, let alone which room, he was in.

He had Krupin cornered. It was time to finish him.

He moved down the carpeted corridor silently. The room in which Kurpin had ducked was straight ahead. He slowed, carefully approaching down the doorway, putting up his pistol and twisting until he brought his back to the wall. Then: light! The rumble of equipment that Cody recognized with sickening slowness. *Elevator!*

He rushed through the doorway just as the doors to the private elevator car closed and Krupin slid down to the parking garage.

Cursing, he turned and sprinted for the door.

# CHAPTER NINE

Down in the van, Sara Durrell twisted the toggle of the rooftop PTZ camera and zoomed in on the figure of the unconscious cop. He still lay where they'd left him, unconscious and handcuffed to a dumpster in the alley across the street. For good measure, Sara had doused him liberally in Bushmills before returning the bottle to its place in the black backpack. She checked her watch.

"Aisha, go ahead and buckle up. Cody should be done in -"

She was interrupted by the roar of an engine and the squealing of tires. Sara's eyes jumped from one monitor to the next, her fingers skimming the keyboard to alert and adjust cameras. The roof unit swiveled and focused just in time to catch the tail end of a Lamborghini fishtail out of the underground parking garage. It straightened itself with a shrieking of brakes and took off down Krasnoskaya Prospect in the direction of the river.

Then the lobby doors of the Tower flew wide and Cody emerged, sprinting toward the van. Sara slid behind the wheel and spun the ignition key. He hauled open the passenger door.

"Krupin's escaped! He -!"

"I'm on it!" She shifted gears and the van leapt out of park. Like the Epsilon now burning on the roof, the van was borrowed. Although ungainly in appearance, the replica Rostelecom vehicle came equipped with the latest, greatest in turbocharged transmission. The engine growled like a locomotive in high gear, its din rising a semi-tone as Sara speed-shifted and floored the accelerator.

"Want me to take the wheel?" joked Cody.

"Funny guy. I outscored you in Tactical Driving by fifteen points!"

"If God had intended women to drive..."

"He obviously did!"

"There!" From her seat behind them, Aisha pointed. "He's heading to that marina!"

The Lambo's taillights jounced and shimmied, slaloming under an entrance sign in Cyrillic. Cody saw rows of piers lit up beneath halogen lights, the white gleam of yachts and the dark-hulls of the scows that worked the side-canals of the Moscow River. He knew the maze of canals eventually spilled into the Volga and, from there, the Black Sea. If Krupin's yacht had the equipment, he could be out of Moscow – and even Russia itself – in short order.

Sara braked to a halt behind the darkened Lamborghini and killed the ignition. The distant figure of Krupin was visible sprinting toward the end of a pier. Docked there was an ultra-modern cabin cruiser - a streamlined double-decker with twin racing screws. A boat with that much horsepower would leave most pursuers sucking its backwash. Krupin reached the dock's end and began unmooring.

"Here!" Cody grasped Sara's elbow and steered her toward a nearby jetty. "Looks like fortune has smiled on us for once."

His words, she reflected, were an understatement. She followed him down the ladder, breathing a prayer that modern Moscow's prosperity had made it possible for someone to purchase a boat like the one they were about to steal.

The ultra-sleek Tecnomar was the last word in cutting-edge sporting craft. Custom manufactured at a price-tag of $3 million (USD), the luxury speedboat sported twin MAN-built 24.2 liter V-12 diesel engines that exerted 4000 horsepower. With its aerodynamic hull and state-of-the-art propulsion and guidance systems, the Tecnomar was capable of running at 60 knots, making it one of the fastest boats on the planet.

"How's your Cyrillic?" Cody asked Sara, gesturing to the stern.

"Her name is *Akhmatova,*" replied Sara. "Like the poet."

"I'm not up on my Russian poets. Was she good?"

"The Commies hated her."

"Reason enough to steal this boat. Let's go."

Down the pier, Krupin's yacht coughed to life and surged away from the pier.

Cody knelt by *Akhmatova's* control console and dug out his cellphone. As expected, a ship like the Tecnomar came with a biometric ignition key. The owner unlocked and started the engine by pressing his thumb to a glass square beside the wheel. Cody probed under the dash until he found a data port, connected his phone and called up an app labeled EN[Y]GMA_7. In moments, the NSA cyber-tool identified and unlocked the yacht's ignition protocol and the Tecnomar hummed to life.

They blasted from the dockside in a spray of foam. Cody twisted the wheel, one eye on the fleeing yacht. A moment later they were pointed in the direction of the canal and hot on Krupin's tail.

# CHAPTER TEN

THE YACHT HAD a time and distance advantage, but its engines were no match for the Tecnomar's. The twin diesel screws, mounted and shielded within their heavy covers, raised barely a purr as the speedboat knifed through the chop.

The Moscow Canals were deceptively named. The word "canal" suggests a narrow thoroughfare, with a tight draft and limited room to maneuver, but Moscow's were nothing like that. Here was a wide waterway with high embankments. By night, it was a shadowy serpent winding through the glittering jewel of lit high rises and the backlit onion domes of traditional Russian cathedrals.

"We're gaining on him!" Sara cried. Beside her, Aisha sat clutching the chicken bar affixed to her seat.

"He's definitely heading somewhere," said Cody. "Any ideas on where?"

"I got nothing." Sara shook her head. "Krupin is not a Moscow boy originally. And he doesn't own any waterfront properties that we know of. So it's probably a *mefiya* bolt hole he's headed for."

"We need to get him before he gets there!"

The *Akhmatova* was making good time. The narrow glow of Krupin's stern lights broadened until the back of his boat loomed large in the canal ahead of them. They had come to a section where the watery labyrinth widened into a sort of lake. Cody saw the tall structures and narrow piers of lakefront development. By the glimmer of nearby streetlamps, he made out the shapes of cafe terraces, patio tables and ungainly pedal-boats moored at their berthings. This part of Moscow was a recreation center and hopping hot-spot during the warmer months. Now, in late autumn, it was a quaint midway to drop in for a meal and drinks but, after hours, nothing more.

They burst out of the canals and into the main thoroughfare of the Moscow River itself. The waterway cut through the center of the city, linking new and old Russia across a series of bridges, some of which dated from the Czar's time. Knowing and navigating this river was a specialist's job, and Krupin seemed to have the aptitude.

Cody saw a bridge up ahead – one of the historic, arching latticework bridges of traditional Moscow. There was a vehicle parked at the near end with its lights on. Krupin had steered his yacht toward the embankment.

"He's arranged a pick-up!" Sara's hand came to his shoulder and clenched.

He grasped the throttle and slammed it forward. There was no way he would permit Krupin to slip through his fingers! Not having come this close. The *Akhmatova* tilted back, nose up, roaring right on the tail of Krupin's yacht. The Russian, visible as a dim shadow in the bridge by the conning tower, jerked left as he steered abruptly away from the embankment. Cody slalomed right, putting himself and the speedboat between Krupin and the embankment.

"When we get close to shore, jump!" he barked.

Sara, intuiting his intention, grabbed Aisha's wrist and dragged her to the rail. Krupin, meanwhile, was swinging his yacht around for another try at the shore. Seeing the *Akhmatova's* running lights ahead of him, he paused in a spray of spume and backwash. Waiting.

Cody steered the speedboat into the shallows. Sara and Aisha slipped over the rail into the knee-deep water and began wading to the embankment, Sara drawing her sidearm as she went. *Good,* he thought. Having her covering fire would make his plan that much more workable.

But for now, he had Krupin to settle with.

Cody eyed the running lights and glaring search beam Krupin had activated just to make things tough on him. But this wouldn't make much difference. His plan was radical in the extreme.

Krupin's voice blasted over the boat's loudspeaker, its huge volume casting the Russian as some giant, angry river god:

"*So. You want to play chicken? Or chess, hey? Bobby Fisherman?*"

Jack Cody's left hand dropped to the throttle while his right twitched above the holstered Browning.

He was among the most trusted of America's clandestine operatives. His accomplishments in the field of special warfare, and the immense trust he had earned from the intelligence community had bought him the top slot in covert ops. He was The President's Man – an operative of formidable capability entrusted with the most sensitive access, close to the center of power, tasked with bringing force of violence against the direst enemies of the state. This job required resilience, judgment and – above all – self-control.

But there was another side to him, the side of a father that had lost both wife and children in one fell swoop. Since their immolation in a car-bomb intended for him, Jack Cody had stalked through the world with a strange, cavalier indifference to survival. In his own mind, he was already dead, more spectre than soldier. He performed his lethal duties with absolute resignation, the likelihood of survival never factoring into his operational calculus. He took huge risks and prevailed. For this, he was deemed lethally efficient. And known by a nickname.

Suicide Cody.

He shoved the throttles forward and hurtled toward the yacht full speed.

# CHAPTER ELEVEN

No sooner had Sara and Aisha splashed ashore than a figure emerged from the waiting vehicle. Sara could discern the shape of the carbine he held in the glow of headlights. A moment later, the figure was scuttling down the embankment, the nose of the rifle wavering in their direction.

"Get down!" Sara hissed, pushing Aisha to the ground. She moved to her left, purposely drawing the armed man away from the girl. Behind her, the speedboat's engine growled and the yacht's chuffa-chuffa'd in response as Cody and Krupin played out their game of move and countermove in the canal.

The figure raised the carbine and fired. The shot went wide, but it was close enough to drive Sara to the ground. Her movement drew the gunman's attention and he fired again, the bullet kicking up a spume of dirt close to her ear.

Sara grasped her automatic in both hands, aimed and fired. The bullet tore the man's leg off at the knee. He lost his carbine and went down with a scream, grasping his shattered leg. The smell of torn flesh and blood — gouts of it — reached Sara's nostrils.

Sara stood. From the look of things, the man had either come alone or his backup had fled. She walked over to him calmly, staring down at the Russian gunsel narrowly.

*"Pomaginya!"* he whispered, his breath ragged.

"You want my help?" Sara smiled and raised her pistol. "I'll help you out of this world, *tovarich.*"

She fired a single bullet into the man's forehead, ending his problems in this life. A moment later, Aisha was grasping her sleeve.

"Look!" she gasped.

Sara turned as the speedboat's engine suddenly roared.

# CHAPTER TWELVE

FOR A MOMENT, Egor Krupin could not believe his eyes. The racing boat had overtaken him - even outmaneuvered him, its captain seizing the opportunity to place himself between Krupin and the shore, blocking access to the getaway team he had arranged. And now, in the final exchange of position and counter-position ...

*He's going to ram the hull!*

A sickening dread tingled within Krupin as he jerked the wheel to port, doing all he could to avoid the slicing nose of the Tecnomar. But the smaller, faster craft rammed Krupin's yacht straight amidships and tore a gaping hole in the hull. The yacht shuddered with impact, its deck rail crumpling and the glass in the wheel-house windows shattering. Krupin was hurled sideways to the deck, where he fell amongst a shower of glass.

The two conjoined boats, screws working against each other, spiraled in a slow and ever-widening circle toward the center of the river. *What kind of man would opt for such an insane tactic?* Krupin wondered. As he reached for the drawer where he kept a spare gun, he found he had to pull himself along using handrails. The deck was tilting. The yacht was taking on water.

Grappling open the drawer, Krupin seized the GSh-18 semi-automatic pistol inside, chambered a round and waited to repel boarders.

# CHAPTER THIRTEEN

AFTER IMPACT, Cody raised the Browning and peppered the shattered bridge with a salvo. Glass snapped and a light bulb popped under the fusillade.

He vaulted over the windshield to the splintered remains of the *Akhmatova's* foredeck. From there, he could peer into the shattered guts of Krupin's yacht. The Tecnomar had punched a hole the size of an SUV in the yacht's side, revealing the engines and electrical housing. Both were slightly elevated from the deck and still operational, but the waterline was slowly creeping higher. As he watched, the rising tide covered and shorted out a power relay, killing it in a spray of sparks.

*Only a matter of time before the whole works shudder to a stop,* he thought. Then he took two big steps, leapt and grasped the yacht's deck rail. Hauling himself up, he tucked and rolled over, coming down onto the deck and drawing the Browning as he rose. He saw movement in the wheelhouse and ducked just as Krupin spun and fired.

Cody threw himself to the deck. The bullet whined

off a hatch. He aimed from a prone position and got off two shots before something gave belowdecks with a loud *snap!* and the lights went out.

The engines continued to churn. The yacht spiraled in its death dance, now noticeably lower in the water.

Cody went to his knees and moved laterally, toward the opposite side of the deck. The *Akhmatova* had rammed the yacht to starboard, damaging herself. She was taking on water and dragging the larger ship down with her. Now on the port side, shrouded in darkness, he could make out the silhouette of the shattered wheelhouse. And, swinging on its hinges, the door into it from the port side. Krupin had fired and fled. There was nowhere else for him to go but forward to the prow.

Below, the engines began to groan in their difficulty. And the stern of the ship slipped lower into the canal. She had begun her final journey to the depths.

A gunshot. Krupin was panicking now, firing blind. Cody maintained his cool and kept low, creeping forward until he could put his back to the wheelhouse. Another gunshot. In the interval following, he raised his eyes above the level of the window and squinted into the gloom.

There by the prow was the silhouette of Krupin. The man was struggling with what looked like an inflatable raft. He would mess with it for a second or two before spinning back, gun raised, not taking any chances, waiting for Cody to appear. As Cody watched, Krupin snapped off another shot.

*So that's his game,* he thought. *Keep me pinned down with random fire while he effects another escape.*

Not this time.

He waited until Krupin's attention was down on the raft before coming out of hiding and moving forward.

He came within a dozen paces of the man. Raised his pistol…

The rising water in the engine room choose that moment to swamp the engine housing. With a groan like the dying whinny of an iron horse, the engine screeched to a halt. And something, somewhere, exploded.

Cody was knocked sprawling by the concussion. Flames mushroomed up through the deck. That section of the yacht not already underwater began to burn. Krupin was crouched by the prow. Cody came to his knees and aimed the Browning, but it was unnecessary.

The Russian had dropped his gun. Somehow, during his wrestling match with the inflatable raft, he had grasped a section of chain affixed to the rail – most probably to steady himself. But the force of the explosion, the shuddering and contortions of the sinking ship had combined to off-balance him. In his twisting skid he had become entangled in the chain and now fought to free himself.

Cody rose calmly and moved forward, keeping Krupin covered with the Browning.

The yacht was now tilted at a 45-degree angle, its nose pointing into the darkened sky. The flames from below deck intensified, fleeing upward to avoid the water, swallowing the wheelhouse and remaining deck planks.

"HELP ME!" Krupin implored.

"Maybe," replied Cody. He stopped six feet short of the man. Spotting Krupin's weapon on the deck, he kicked it backward into the fire before leveling the Browning, its sight bisecting the Russian's forehead. "What's Vetrov got up his sleeve?"

"I tell you everything! Everything! Just! PLEASE!"

Krupin, his cool completely shattered, rattled his chains like a comic book ghost. A section of flame had crawled toward him. Planking flaked beneath his left foot. Smoke and steam slithered ever closer.

"You tell me everything now or you die."

"Okay! Okay!" Krupin held up his free hand, throwing a frantic glance at the dancing fire. "I don't know everything! But he is calling it Operation CERBERUS. He is moving something from a weapon stockpile in Pochep! Bryansk Oblast!"

"Moving *what?*"

"I don't know!" Krupin yanked his foot from an erupting tongue of flame. "I arrange they meet in France! Monte Carlo!"

"When?" Despite the encroaching inferno, Cody kept his voice cool and level.

"Three days from now! Is all I know! Is everything I know! Now ... *HELP ME!*"

Cody felt heat on the back of his neck and looked over his shoulder. The flames had crawled up and around, isolating Krupin in a shrinking oval of fire. The hem of his jacket was smouldering. Flames jumped and danced close enough to cause him to wiggle around for relief.

"I appreciate your help, Mr. Krupin." Cody holstered the Browning.

The blaze was now chewing up Krupin's pant leg. Polyester melted onto his leg as he shrieked, throwing his head back, eyes and teeth clamped.

"I want you to think about that girl, Krupin. You know the one. She died in my arms, you know ..."

Krupin's mouth, wide but soundless, reflected the terror in his eyes. His leg was slow roasting like a rack of lamb. And a weird lambent blue rose from his jacket sleeve. His flesh was being seared alive. *Flame jumps,* Cody noted.

"Please! Help! *Meee!*"

*It really is like a living thing …*

Krupin's leg smouldered. And now his arm was going up like a log in a roaring fireplace. His face, burned black, twisted away and gave one last scream:

*"Please shoot me!"*

"With pleasure," replied Cody. He put a bullet into the screaming ball of fire that was Krupin's head and then vaulted for the rail.

He slipped over into the drink, gasping at the shock of the cold water as it hit. Striking out for shore, Cody kept his eyes fixed on the lights of the vehicle parked at the near end of the bridge. And listened to the yacht's dying shrieks of agony as the flames, and then the river, grasped and devoured her.

# CHAPTER FOURTEEN

Moscow.

Dawn.

A sprinkling of pedestrians dotted the sidewalks of the Fruzenskaya, mostly laborers, factory and hospital workers commuting to early shifts. As was customary in Russia, they moved quickly, each keeping to themselves. Those using public transport queued up in orderly lines at bus stops, eyes down on newspapers or cellphones. The odd burst of traffic swept the road from time to time. Across the Moscow River loomed the white, many-windowed facade of the Russian Ministry of Defense building.

A lone man moved quietly among them. His passage attracted little or no attention. In even this most circumspect of European cities, his presence was ghostly. Middle-aged, of slightly less-than-average height and dressed in a plain down jacket and workman's cloth cap, he was as nondescript as any Moscow laborer heading to work. When he did enter the vision of other travelers, his passage was quickly forgotten, as if he had vanished into the very bricks of the buildings themselves.

The man knew a lot about vanishing. But any attempt to ask him how much would prove difficult. His responses to others, which tended toward vagueness, were always calculated to fit the approach.

Any Russian asking for a light would encounter a clipped affirmative delivered in a perfect Moscow accent and a light offered in the traditional Russian way, one hand cupping the flame. A similarly native response would be encountered by anyone asking for directions in Paris, taking a survey in Berlin or flogging wares on the streets of Rome. Blending in was this man's instinctive specialty – one he had honed to a professional art.

A few blocks past the bus stop, the streets grew shabbier. A sheet of crumpled newspaper blew disconsolately across the sidewalk. A series of tall warehouses loomed over this section of the river, most used to shift wholesale goods in and out of the Federation's capital. At the doorway to the shabbiest and most weathered, the nondescript man stopped and removed a keychain from his pocket. With a glance up and down the street, he let himself in, locking the door behind him.

A small vestibule with chairs and a coatrack lay within. The man removed his jacket and hat, hung them up and then used his keys to open a second door beyond which a sterile concrete hallway stretched toward a bright steel security door. The nondescript man approached, tapped a code into the keypad lock set beside it and smiled as the steel barrier slid aside to reveal an office. With a contented sigh, he took a seat at the desk.

He flipped through the mail, each piece of which was addressed to a different person, none of whom existed.

All were aliases for which the man could produce ID. More than a master of deception and disguise, he was a lifelong chameleon whose actual name was known to fewer than five people on Earth, one of whom was Sara Durrell. To her he was just dear old Uncle Horace.

Horace Parsons had attained the highest rank possible in British intelligence for a man of his social class and temperament. The son of a Liverpool shopkeeper, he had joined MI-6 after a stint in the army and found the work very much to his liking. During his operational career, he had forged a reputation for thoroughness and clever improvisation. And along the way he had befriended an earnest young CIA officer named Craig Durrell.

Their operational partnership became the stuff of legend. Between them, they had effectively coordinated all major western counterintelligence projects in eastern Europe for three decades. Yes, Langley and London had their managers and mandarins (so-called 'controllers') calling the shots. But if you wanted something done quickly and quietly in Moscow or Sarajevo or Kiev, you needed the blessing of Horace and Craig or it just wasn't going to happen.

Craig Durrell had retired to a country club estate in Boca Raton. Horace Parsons, meanwhile, his identity still unknown to the opposition despite decades in the trenches, had chosen a very different place to go to pasture.

He had always liked Moscow.

And so, after assembling a blind of false identities and passports, he had taken up residence there – right in the heart of enemy territory. He had effectively retired out in the cold, the place where he felt most at home.

Given the circumstances, it had come as no great surprise when his old paymasters came knocking with a part-time job. Although retired, Parsons now oversaw the Vicarage – the nickname for this clandestine storehouse of weapons and equipment used jointly by MI-6 and CIA.

And, most recently, by Sara Durrell and Jack Cody.

Parsons' computer chirped. He opened his e-mail to see an urgent message from Sara flashing at the top of his inbox.

Dear Uncle Horace:

We'll stop by when we're in the neighborhood.

Looking forward to a visit.

XO, Sara

Parsons smiled. The message meant that Sara and Cody had been successful in their mission and would be arriving shortly. He rose and exited his office through a side door. The doorway led out to a steel catwalk that ringed a vast warehouse space. Parsons paused with his hands on the railing and surveyed his inventory.

From this vantage, he looked down on a collection of motorcycles and automobiles, racks and cabinets of weapons, stacks of computer equipment and an acre of "wardrobe" – disguises to change an operative into anything from a Chechen peasant to a state security official at staff level. There was even a black Epsilon micro-light – twin to the one now burning atop the Vostok tower. And a parking place for the customized Rost-elecom van he'd loaned them. Casting an eye over all this, Parsons swelled with contented pride. He loved looking over the inventory.

But for now he had more pressing matters. His dear

friend's niece was due to arrive soon with her young man. Parsons shuffled along the catwalk to a narrow doorway that led into a small kitchen. He rummaged in the cabinets for a box of cookies and then set about making tea. Because receiving visitors without offering them a proper cuppa would simply be uncivilized.

# CHAPTER FIFTEEN

THEY APPROPRIATED Krupin's getaway SUV. Keeping to the backstreets, Cody got them within walking distance of the Vicarage. They abandoned the vehicle in the parking lot of a grocery store and hiked toward the river. By the time they reached the Fruzenskaya, the flow of traffic and pedestrians had picked up. Blending in with the morning commute, they gained the doorway of the shabby warehouse where Parsons stood waiting.

"Hello! Do come in ..." The old Brit smiled, blinking owlishly behind his round spectacles as he closed and locked the door behind them. He looked Cody up and down. "You do look a bit wet I daresay, Mr. Cody. Been for a swim?"

"I was forced to take a dip in Moskva." Cody chuckled. "I could do with a change of clothes."

"Coming right up. This way, won't you please?" Parsons conducted them to his cluttered office where they left Sara and Aisha to relax on a frumpy couch then went off to fetch Cody some dry togs. While he changed, Parsons brought in the tea tray and set it on the low table before the couch. Cody joined them and Parsons poured for everyone.

"So!" Parsons stirred his tea. "Seems you've had an exciting few days! Morning radio reports a fire atop the Vostok Tower. And a boat's apparently sunk in the Moskva. This on the heels of this week's panicked comms traffic about you all from Langley and Vauxhall." The older man smiled gently. "Sara, love. Don't you think it's time to tell your dear old Uncle Horace what's going on?"

Cody appreciated the man's diplomacy. The three of them had shown up on his doorstep two days ago. At Sara's request, he had taken them all in without a moment's hesitation. Parsons had provided them with equipment, accommodations and logistical support, no questions asked. He was an old school spook – one of those left over from the hot days of the Cold War who still adhered to its rigid codes of loyalty. Parsons and Sara's uncle had been close for decades. Sara had known the man since age sixteen. That he would help them was a foregone conclusion. That he would protect them on principle alone was welcome news to Cody in the present circumstance.

"We have to stop General Greb Vetrov," Sara said. "That's at the heart of this. Cody was on a mission to cripple the general's arms traffic in stolen nukes. And I was busy tracking down Aisha, here. It turns out that there is some nebulous connection between Vetrov's arms dealings and Aisha. The point of overlap seems to be Thelma Justice, the self-help and women's empowerment guru. But the main reason we came is that the apparatus of CIA has suddenly been turned against us. We're encountering powerful resistance from within the bureaucracy. Jared Parnell is behind it."

Parsons, whose expression had remained neutral throughout all of this, raised his eyebrows at the name. "Jared Parnell?" He sounded incredulous. "The same Jared Parnell whose mismanagement bankrupted the CIA's Istanbul station? Whose incompetence nearly ignited a civil war in the Sudan? 'Fiasco-in-Romania' Parnell? You mean to tell me that insufferable little wanker hasn't been fired yet?"

"Yes."

"That man has single-handedly done more harm to western intelligence efforts than the entire KGB!" Parsons sniffed. He shook his head in disgust. "But you say he's in Langley now? Failed his way up the ladder in typical fashion, I shouldn't wonder. But Vetrov... He's another matter. Very smart. Very dangerous. We've kept an eye on him for years."

"You mean MI-6?" asked Cody.

"Yes. MI-6. CIA. And other... interested parties." Parsons smiled obliquely. "So, you did confide in me that your interest lay in Egor Krupin. Well, yes. He's a known confederate of Vetrov's."

"Was," Cody corrected him. "He's dead now."

"Well done!" Parsons hoisted his cup. "Malignant little man. It's good to be shot of him. So, what did you find out? And more importantly, how can I – how can we – be of help?"

"Before he died, I managed to extract some information from Krupin. Vetrov is still actively trafficking illicit Russian weapons. His latest shipment originates in Pochep, in the Bryansk Oblast. The transaction he is planning is being called Operation CERBERUS. He's to rendezvous with his buyer in Monte Carlo in three days."

"Interesting." Parsons narrowed his eyes. "Pochep is

quite close to the border with Ukraine. I remember hiking past it one day back in the Brezhnev years. Less than 100 km as I recall. Pochep's main function is as a storage and demolition site for chemical munitions. But it's also used to store less conventional items. The operation's code name is telling."

"Cerberus is the name of the three-headed dog who guards the gates of hell in Greek mythology," offered Aisha. "Could it mean multiple attackers?"

"Very possibly." Parsons nodded at her. "Or multiple types of weapons." He returned his attention to Cody. "You'll need assistance once you reach France. Not to mention help getting there. Do you think Monte Carlo will be your final destination?"

"Not likely, no."

"Very well." Parsons sat back. "Backchannel can help."

"Backchannel?" Sara leaned forward, fiercely curious. "You mean it's real?" She turned to Cody. "Have you heard about this?"

"Only rumors." His esteem of Parsons grew. "Stories of a star chamber of retired intelligence officers from the allied countries. A group that observes and guides global intelligence affairs. Elders who keep overwatch, who mentor and correct ... and, occasionally, punish those who transgress. Isn't that right?"

Parsons said nothing.

"Uncle Horace?"

The old Brit glanced at her then smiled. "We've got you on a Finnish diplomatic flight that departs Sheremetyevo day after tomorrow. We've arranged for it to make a detour in Paris. Alain Jacquard will be your liaison in France. His resources are more limited than ours here at the Vicarage, but I'm sure they'll suffice. He can provide you with most anything you need. And whatever happens, don't worry, Mr. Cody. Backchannel has you."

"Thanks."

"On one condition."

Cody raised his eyebrows.

"When all this is over, Parnell is ours." Uncle Horace's smile was cold. "You leave him to us."

Parsons seemed like a nice man. But in that instant, Cody was sure he would never want to get on the old Brit's bad side.

"Deal," he said. "Parnell is yours when this is done. Do your worst."

# CHAPTER SIXTEEN

FROM HIS CORNER office on the fourth floor of the Palazzo del Sant'Uffizio, His Eminence Joseph D'Agostino, SJ looked down upon the Petriano gate to Vatican City. Although not within the borders of the Papal city-state, the Palazzo was considered an extraterritorial protectorate of the Vatican. Since 1525 it had served as the headquarters of the Congregation of the Doctrine of the Faith, originally known as The Inquisition.

The Congregation, like other government organizations, was as prone to acronyms (CDF) as it was to complexity. Beneath its labyrinthine umbrella, the CDF controlled branches to police the teaching of doctrine, profanation of the Sacraments and enforcement of professional conduct. It was to the Congregation that wayward priests and heretics answered. And it was from the CDF that Church enforcers were dispatched. Some were publicly acknowledged, such as Papal legates and investigators. Others, like the ones D'Agostino oversaw, were clandestine. It was for this reason that the Jesuit was most often referred to by his unofficial title: the Black Cardinal.

But for the moment, Cardinal D'Agostino was not pondering any of this. He was remembering his first glimpse of the Petriano gate, when he'd come here as a young prelate back in the early days of President Reagan. So much had changed since then. The Cold War, then in full swing, had been won due in large part to the unorthodox cooperation between the Vatican and the CIA. One by one, the iron walls fell. And the young Catholic priest had grown in his faith and profession, rising to occupy this most prestigious of offices.

A knock came on D'Agostino's door. It was Monsignor Lewis, his personal secretary.

"Your Eminence, we have an after-action report from Washington, DC. The news, I am afraid, is not good." The Monsignor remained standing before the Cardinal's desk as he read from a clipboard. "As instructed, the team attempted an intercept-or-destroy on the target of interest at a public rally in DC. They were unsuccessful. Col. Demaso was killed in the action."

D'Agostino closed his eyes. Bennicio Demaso had served the CDF loyally as head of its action service team for over a decade. His loss, and the compromise of the team, was devastating.

"So the action was a dead loss, then?" D'Agostino asked. "The princess remains at large? As does the artifact?"

"Correct, Your Eminence. None of the mission objectives were achieved. And the Guard team is completely compromised."

"Very well. Thank you, monsignor. Please be so kind as to lay in a call to Father Valachi at the abbey in Torino and inform me when he is on the line."

"At once, Your Eminence." The monsignor bowed and left.

D'Agostino rose from his desk and returned to the window. Outside, the sun was beginning its descent and the Vatican streets were awash in orange and shadow. D'Agostino's mood was unsettled but showed outward calm. His orders from the Curia were explicit and clear as regards the item currently in the Princess Aisha's possession. His first wave had failed to capture or destroy the item and its holder. So more extreme measures were needed.

The phone rang on the Cardinal's desk. He answered. Monsignor Lewis announced that he had Father Valachi on the line. D'Agostino asked that the call be put through and any interruptions held in abeyance until further notice.

"Father Valachi? It's Cardinal D'Agostino. *Dominus vobiscum,* good father. All is well at your abbey?"

"All is well, your eminence." Valachi's voice was soft, almost whispery. Despite the robust connection, D'Agostino strained to listen.

"It had befallen us that our brother in Christ Col. Demaso has been lost."

"Mercy upon him."

"God grant him eternal rest. Father, I fear I shall have to call upon the brothers of the Order of St. Adrian."

"We stand ready, your eminence."

"Very well. Have them stage up at once. And I shall require your presence here at Vatican City. I'll send a helicopter. You'll have a late supper with me here in my offices, when I shall relay your orders."

"Very good, your eminence."

D'Agostino clicked off and then contacted Lewis

who re-arranged some items on the schedule before ordering a delivery dinner with his usual efficiency. Two meetings were re-scheduled and one pushed forward. D'Agostino sat for two hours with a fellow Jesuit, a monsignor from the office of professional conduct. That final duty discharged, he watched as Lewis set the table in the private dining room, then busied himself with paperwork until a soft knock came at around 8 PM.

"Your eminence, Father Valachi is here."

"Very good." D'Agostino sighed and removed his glasses. "Monsignor, pray fetch the good father in. You may serve us our first course and then depart for the day."

"Thank you, your eminence."

D'Agostino rose and awaited his guest. Monsignor Lewis opened the door for him and then stood back.

Father Uriel Valachi, head of the Order of St. Adrian, entered the office. He was a spare, rangey-looking man in his mid-forties. His thick, dark hair was starting to gray and the lines of premature worry were etched into his weathered brown face. A scar ran from his right eyebrow to a point halfway down his cheek. He wore a black shirt with a clerical collar, black pants and blazer. On the blazer's front pocket was the arms of his order. He stepped forward, accepted the Cardinal's hand and bowed his head.

"Come, father. I have ordered us some supper." D'Agostino conducted them to the private dining nook. Monsignor Lewis came pushing a trolley containing their meal. He served their salads and wine before departing, closing the door softly behind him.

"Your men are staged up?" asked D'Agostino.

"They are, your eminence," replied Valachi in his clipped, hoarse whisper. "We await your orders."

"Excellent. You shall pick up where Col. Demasso and his men failed." D'Agostino's voice betrayed real grief. "Since the 1600s, your order has repeatedly proven itself the Church's most effective clandestine force. For this reason, by Papal decree, we call on you rarely. Only in situations most dire, where survival of Christ's church is at stake. This is such a case."

"What exactly is the threat, your eminence?"

"One of our most closely-guarded secrets. It falls to me to share this secret with you. I do so now with the instructions that you conduct your mission without sharing this information with anyone, including your closest lieutenants. You are familiar, of course, with the Knights of the Temple."

"The Templars. Of course."

D'Agostino nodded. "The story of the Templars' betrayal of the Holy Father and subsequent punishment by the Church is well-known. What is not wholly understood by most are the deeper reasons. During their stay in Jerusalem, the Templars were resident upon Jerusalem's Temple Mount. While there, they came into possession of a number of relics. You are of course familiar with the Dead Sea Scrolls..."

"I am, your eminence," said Valachi. "A series of Biblical verses transcribed on parchment by desert monks living in caves near Qumran. They offer a heretical view of some Jewish teachings."

"Indeed. But the Qumran community was not alone in curating ancient records. Nor did they necessarily limit themselves to their own transcriptions. Or to parchment."

Valachi sat listening, silent and unmoving. His was the preternatural stillness of the predator. Even the Black Cardinal found it unsettling. Nevertheless he continued:

"While on the Mount, the initial group of nine Templar knights made several discoveries, one of which was a clay tablet written in Aramaic. When the tablet was translated and studied by the Templars, it was understood to hold a secret that would make them invincible against their foes. The Templars began to modify their military practices in accordance with the teachings on this tablet, which purported to be a version of the Book of Genesis. The Templars went on to win many military victories because of this."

"I see, your eminence."

"But where they fell into error – the error that led to their excommunication and sentencing by the Holy Father – was when they used this tablet to modify their worship and religious observances. They fell into heresy, Father Valachi. A heresy that has returned to our world."

"Indeed?"

"The tablet has resurfaced after centuries of obscurity. Father Demaso and his team were sent to recover the tablet and its current owner. It was during that mission that he and his men were killed. Their mission is now yours. Where he failed, you must not."

"I understand, your eminence. A question, if I may. What does the tablet say that is so controversial?"

D'Agostino told him. And although his outer demeanor remained stoic, Father Valachi's mouth went dry at the Cardinal's words and sweat beaded on his forehead.

# CHAPTER SEVENTEEN

THE NEXT MORNING, Cody sat nursing a glass of tea and studying the entrance to the Beletoz Building from a cafe across the street. The address, which housed a post office as well as the Moscow offices of the Order of World Harmony, was located in a busy section of downtown near the Patriarch's Palace and Dominion Cathedral. The neighborhood was tourist country – the kind of locale wherein informal meetings could be rounded out with a walking tour of the local sites. From where Cody sat, the spires of the Kremlin were visible above the skyline in the middle distance. The flow of traffic on the street, both automotive and pedestrian, was brisk.

In keeping with its role as a *mefiya* front, the Beletoz was ultra-modern. Moscow was a mix of stately historic and contemporary architecture, onion domes intermixed with the sort of glass and chrome construction more commonly associated with a place like Dallas or London. The stamp of *mefiya* money was visible in the facades of these new buildings – a thumbing of the nose at the past by the up-and-coming money of the new Federation.

*But some things never change in Russia,* Cody noted. There was a security guard at the lobby doors, lolling indolently behind his desk, barely taking notice of passersby. Cody knew the building staff would be careless about theft or intrusion. As was the practice in Russia, organizations within the Beletoz would arrange their own security rather than trust the landlords to provide umbrella protection. Tenants with any assets of value to protect would hire their own guards. Cody intended to exploit this lack of consistency to its full potential. He rose and paid for his tea.

"Thank you, father," said the old woman behind the counter.

"You are welcome my child," said Cody in Russian, brushing dust from the sleeve of his priest's cassock. "Bless you."

He exited the cafe, angling toward the building entrance. He caught sight of Aisha moving along the sidewalk by herself. A dozen paces behind her, Sara shadowed the princess' progress.

As arranged, all three met at the lobby doors at the same time. Pretending not to know one another, they coagulated in a small traffic jam. Both Cody and Sara stepped back, allowing Aisha to enter first. To the security guard, it appeared as nothing more than simple courtesy. But it was part of their strategy to keep Aisha covered while inside.

The bottom floor of the Beletoz was configured like a small shopping mall, with boutique stores lining the lobby and first floor. Aisha moved down the marbled and mirrored main concourse. The post office facility was set up like a retail outlet. A counter in back served as a drop-off and point of sale hub. Racks of envelopes and post-cards lined the right-hand wall. Stacks of PO boxes covered the left. Aisha took up station behind the one woman waiting in line. Sara stood directly behind her. Cody drifted to the racks and pretended to peruse postcards.

He kept one eye on the two women and another on the door. Outside the post office, patrons shuffled through the lobby. Another security guard, from the same company as the one at the door, ambled by in a distracted patrol. Cody was about to breathe easy when he caught sight of a second, unexpected guard. She appeared from out of nowhere, suddenly visible among the crowd. In a flash, he recognized a uniformed figure from the Furies of Harmony, Thelma Justice's personal guard.

*Armed, too,* Cody noted. In Russia, private armed security was a rarity that was strictly controlled by the state. That Thelma Justice could have her own armed guards moving at large through a public space was unprecedented. Unlike the rent-a-cop, the Fury moved carefully, eyes sweeping every detail of the lobby. She looked into the post office outlet. Cody's heart skipped a beat when she stopped and squinted, apparently drawn by the sight of Aisha.

Cody dropped the postcard in his hand and hustled over to the Fury, spreading his arms and allowing a wide, goofy smile to cross his face.

"Ah! Perhaps you can help me?" he said in loud Russian, affecting the accent of somebody from Rostov-on-Don. In Moscow, such folk were considered backwards yokels. "I am looking for something."

The Fury, startled by his sudden approach, knitted her brow in confusion. As Cody suspected, she spoke little if any Russian.

"Ah!" He put his hands on is thighs and bent

forward, as though thinking. "Uh ... Thel - ma? Juss-tiss?"

At this, the Fury's brow uncurled. Thelma's was a name she knew.

"Where?" Cody asked, as though patiently reasoning with someone who spoke no Russian.

The Fury sighed, torn between whatever suspicion had stopped her in her tracks and her orders to help anyone requesting assistance regarding the Order of World Harmony. She sighed, took a final glance into the post office, and then beckoned Cody to follow her. They boarded an elevator. She punched the button for the fourth floor. Cody kept up a babbling stream of nonsense, describing how excited he was to come to Moscow and how impressive he found the sites. The Fury kept nodding uncomfortably, pretending to understand. But by the time they got off the elevator, it was obvious to Cody she did not.

They followed a carpeted office hallway to a suite identified as belonging to the Order of World Harmony by the Cyrillic lettering on the nameplate beside the office door. But as Cody approached, a workman emerged pushing a trolley cart, atop which was a filing cabinet. The reception area was vacant except for a single office swivel chair and the evenly spaced rectangle impressions in the carpet left by recently removed office furniture. It was clear the Order was bugging out.

Cody made a show of surprise, only half of which was make-believe.

# CHAPTER EIGHTEEN

"HALLO!" Parsons shuffled into the Vicarage's small kitchen, intent on a midnight snack. Clad in housecoat, pajamas and slippers, he had expected to find no one present. A few hours earlier, he had sent his guests off to their respective quarters to rest up before tomorrow's flight. And so he was surprised to find Aisha sitting at the table, eyes down on a wrapped package before her.

"You alright, dear?" He paused while opening the fridge. The girl looked to be unsettled.

Her eyes met his. She said nothing.

"Hunh ..." Parsons fetched out a block of cheese. "I was about to have some toasted cheese. Care for some?" He squinted at the box in front of her. "That's the package you mailed to yourself?"

She nodded.

"Some sort of ... tablet, is it?" Parsons spoke as he toasted bread. "I'm a bit fuzzy on the details. An artifact of some type, I think Cody said."

Another long silence. Parsons recognized the

numbing effect of delayed shock. The girl, despite her ability to handle herself, had been through a lot these past days. *Finally securing the package must be a weight off her shoulders,* he thought, retrieving and melting cheese over the toast. He whipped up a few slices, put them on a plate and took a seat across from her. For a long moment, he assumed she wouldn't eat. But soon her arm snaked out and grasped a slice in her fingers.

"Thank you, Mr. Parsons," she whispered.

"You're most welcome, dear." He smiled. "Are you ... alright? Is there anything you'd like to talk about? I may be old, but I'm a rather good listener. And more than happy to help."

Aisha said nothing for a long moment. Finishing her toast, she brushed crumbs from her fingertips and touched the brown wrapping paper of the parcel in front of her.

"There are many names for it," she began quietly. "Ancient scholars called it 'the Marian Fragment' or the 'Hidden Gospel.' It has disappeared and resurfaced many times throughout history. Islamic scholars were the first to examine it. Then it vanished during the Crusades. Rumors of Templar involvement were spoken. Then Spanish scholars got their hands on it some time during the Reconquista. They had it briefly before it was recaptured by the noble warriors of Islam. We found the tablet in the deserts of my Emirate, possibly lost from a diplomatic caravan during the Middle Ages."

Parsons listened, transfixed.

"The people of Judea had ink and various types of skins and papyrus on which to write. But this was done in clay, using a stylus. Primitive. The language is Aramaic - the language Jesus spoke. It was from his time. From a community outside of Jerusalem. The Desert Rabbis. They who rejected all the baggage imported into Judaism by the Pharisees and Herod's government. They lived simply, in caves in the hills around Jerusalem. They were such a small presence that the Roman authorities didn't even bother with them. Left them alone. Isolated in their solitude."

"And what did they do?"

"Out there in the desert, they worshipped and prayed and studied God. And they gave shelter to passersby and those lost in the desert. This fragment tells of one such traveler. The tablet begins with the words: 'In that season we offered refuge to Yeshua, rabbi from Galilee, who remained with us and taught for three days.'"

Parsons sat motionless. It took him a moment to realize he had stopped breathing.

"On one side of the tablet is a record of a sermon Jesus gave in which he taught about the Book of Genesis. He makes reference to events not recorded in the Bible and offers stern words about the proper relationship between man and woman. These words... were not popular with Islamic scholars of Crusader Days."

"Why?" Parsons was surprised. "I would expect the attitudes of women in their time to be rather the same as in the time of Jesus. Same geographic location, more or less. Similar cultures ..."

"Because the attitudes of Jesus towards women were not typical for his time." Aisha's voice was firm. "This is reflected in the teachings. And confirmed by the inscription on the back side of the tablet. It is in Latin, rendered and signed by the Templar knight who discovered it."

"Extraordinary! And who was this remarkable knight?"

Aisha trembled. "Her name," she said, "was the Lady Roxanne of Burgundy."

# CHAPTER NINETEEN

EVERYTHING WAS GOING PERFECTLY.

Thelma Justice savored the view from the balcony of her chalet above Monte Carlo. She caught a whiff of Aspen on the breeze that blew in and jangled the wind-chimes behind her and felt a slight chill crowding the edge of the night. Beyond the balustrade glimmered the lights of the city. Hers was an idyllic bower in which to play. And plot. With the imminent arrival of her guest, she planned to do plenty of both.

The plotting was what she felt best about at this particular moment. As leader of the Order of Divine Harmony, hers was a heavy load. Women all over the planet looked to her as guide and role model. Given her ubiquitous popularity among women, it would be fair to say she held the destiny of half the planet in her hands. Now she was determined to do something about the other half.

*What good is having power if you never use it?* she asked herself, chuckling. She took a sip of expensive Italian wine and tilted her nose into the wind.

She controlled the women. And in her lover Greb Vetrov, she had found her perfect counterpart - a wild and dangerous Alpha male, a lover fit to command her armies as a general and lead conquests in her name. She would need that kind of power for what came next. Once they had located Aisha and relieved her of the treasure.

*The Tablet ...*

Thelma Justice had read every book on the subject, consulted every living expert on the artifact and used a spirit medium to contact a few of the dead ones. She knew the fragment contained the missing element she needed to put her plan into motion, the element that would draw skeptical women off the fence about supporting her and change the hearts of those who actively opposed her.

*Scratch a wine-mom feminist and you'll find a power-hungry jackal,* Thelma thought.

Power. It was every woman's secret desire, the magical golden apple that inspired every female quest. And it was upon the goal of power that Thelma Justice kept her eye firmly fixed. Unlike men, she did not covet it as an end in itself but rather as a medium via which she could induce change in the world. It was not the power but what she could do with it that inspired her so. Just the thought...

*Justice Power,* she told herself. And smiled.

For far too long, men had ruled. They, like women, were prisoners of their biology. But unlike women, they could not control it. Their destructive impulses had manifested in a million or more wars, murders and rapes committed across the span of history. With the advent of nuclear weapons, it was now clear they could no longer be entrusted to control their aggressive instincts. The sign and seal of the mushroom cloud was the Omega on their primacy. It was time for them to relinquish their hold and let women rule.

*It's not only logical*, she thought. *It's natural.* Organic in the way seasons turning from one to another are organic. And, whether they liked it or not, the seasons *would* turn. She, Master of the Order of World Harmony, would see to it, her crusade impelled by the excellent violence of the Alpha whose chain she held in her gloved fist.

She smiled at the image of her lover as a snarling jackal.

*Summer is over. It is time for autumn to take hold.*

Headlights cut the darkness below. A limousine passed through her estate's gates. Her heart began to beat a little faster, sweat prickling her temples and wrists. He was back – the man who slaked her passion and with the help of whose hands she cradled the world.

There was an elevator that brought residents up from the garage level into the kitchen. She waited by its door, wrapped in a negligee and nothing else. Her heart sped up when she heard the door rumble closed and the motor whir. He was coming closer to her moment by moment. Then the car stopped, the door parted and he was there.

Thelma Justice stepped forward and wrapped Greb Vetrov in her arms. The thick set, bald Russian grappled her to him and grunted, pleased himself. Then his hands began traveling, exploring beneath the negligee's soft, knotted folds, caressing her satiny stomach and ass. She responded by purring and curling in closer to him. His mouth sought hers. She laughed, evading his kiss for a long moment before their lips met. A lingering hungry kiss shuddered between them. As he finished and pulled away, her teeth grasped his lower lip and pulled hard enough to draw blood.

Vetrov growled and threw her to the ground. She landed on the carpeted hallway with a thud and then suddenly he was thrashing atop her, pushing aside the folds of her lace teddy and probing with blunt hands. Face, stomach, breasts. He meant to have all of her.

Ever the she-wolf, she responded by attacking his clothes. A howl of need rose within her and she tore at his shirt, reducing it to shreds as she undressed him with fiery desperation. What was it about the man that drove her to such rages? Greb Vetrov was every man she had ever fantasized about and then some. She attacked his belt, undoing and pulling it free. Vetov seized it from her, doubled it and smacked her flank hard leaving a red welt.

She bared her teeth and sank them into his chest, drawing blood. Delighted, he flung her on her back, parted her legs and entered her. She opened to receive him, gasping and thrashing, pulling him toward and into her, impaling herself on him. Soon she was gasping his name, her mind filling with his scent, the roughness of his presence. Greb Vetrov… *her* man!

Afterwards, with the vodka drinks she prepared for them in hand, they sipped and snuggled. And planned.

"All went well in the Ukraine," he told her. "We encountered no resistance. My team was able to enter and leave the facility at Pochep with the Easter eggs secure in the basket. The highest-ranking man there was a sergeant. He even detailed men to come and help me load the truck."

Thelma sipped and hummed a satisfaction that came from deep within her. So her Alpha male had secured the stick. Now all that remained left was for them to locate the carrot.

"The time has come, my dear one, for me to tell you everything." She drained her vodka glass and set it on the bedside table of her luxurious bedroom. She sat up and lit a stick of incense, placing it in an elaborate clay holder by the bed. The scent of jasmine flowered in the room. She returned to his hard, naked body and fit herself into him.

"The one constant in history, my love, is change." Her tone took on a hypnotic, incantatory cadence. Even the strong-willed Vetrov found himself beguiled by her voice. "Summer passes to autumn. So the age of man passes. To the age of woman. It's time. It's long *past* time, in fact. People always used to speak of how women tended to be smaller. Weaker. Unfit to fight and lead. But that has all evened out in the era of technology. A woman with a gun in her purse is superior to a half-dozen unarmed attackers. Power is no longer a case of overwhelming and bearing down. No, in our time, power is a case of locating the fulcrum and applying pressure in the right way at just the right moment. That is how we intend to seize this moment. This is how the age of woman will be born."

Vetrov listened, not watching her as she spoke. She knew this was how he focused. He waited until she finished before speaking. "When you have power, someone always is seeking to take it away," he reminded her.

"When you find Cody and the princess Aisha, when you locate the tablet, we will have everything we need."

"This tablet. Why so important?" Vetrov sat up in bed, drained his vodka and searched the room with his eyes for a refill. "With the easter eggs I have brought, you can make any demands you want."

"With the fragment on the tablet, I can change people's understanding." She spoke patiently. "The most powerful weapon is belief. And it's the one we have the best chance of affecting."

"Most people believe in God," Vetrov said.

"What if I can change their understanding of God?"

He found this surprising enough to be taken aback. "And this tablet? It can help you do this?"

"It helped an entire order of Christian knights see the world differently and changed the way they fought and worshipped. The tablet made them the most invincible and wealthiest order of knights in their time. Theirs was the most powerful organization in the civilized world."

Vetrov listened, spellbound.

"Get me that tablet and I'll do it again," she vowed. "The world is there for the taking, my lover. And I will make it mine."

# CHAPTER TWENTY

CODY, Sara and Aisha departed Moscow without incident aboard a Finnish C-130. The flight landed in Helsinki and they walked off the ramp of the transport and directly aboard a FedEx courier jet for the run to Paris. Parsons' preparations had been meticulous – the plane's crew didn't even give them a second look.

Aisha and Sara dozed during the uneventful flight. They were greeted as they stepped off the plane in Paris by a frowning, elderly man wearing a fedora, top coat and scarf. Like Parsons, he blinked at them from behind lenses albeit of a different style. Alain Jacquard favored thick black frames and a gruff, almost rude frankness.

"So this is your party? Only three? I see." Jacquard sighed as though disapproving. He bent to pick up one of Sara's suitcases. "Well, we shall have to make do. Are you tired of flying yet?"

"Exhausted," Sara admitted. "We're glad to be on the ground."

"For a few minutes, anyway." Jacquard turned and walked at a swift clip, not glancing behind to see if they kept up, toward a small, private terminal. He spoke brusquely and quickly: "We're boarding a flight to Monte Carlo. Our expected travel time is about an hour-and-a-half. I suppose you are hungry. Americans are always hungry. It's because nobody's ever taught you how to eat properly. Never mind. I shall have food delivered to the terminal."

Cody was about to say no need, but by then Jacquard had grappled a cellphone from his pocket and begun arguing loudly in French with somebody at the other end of the line. The argument continued through the doorway and into the musty waiting area of the private terminal. Cody paused and gazed around the carpeted lounge. It was like the arrival/departure bay of any large airport but in miniature. Dust motes climbed through diagonal shafts of light that fell in through the skylight. There was even a small ticket counter behind which stood a young French air force enlisted officer. She waited as Jacquard finished his call and hung up with an angry grunt before starting to yell at the enlisted officer. Cody admired her self-control as she stood listening without batting an eyelash. When he was done, she lifted a radio mic to her lips and spoke into the PA system. An announcement in French. Personnel began moving quickly through the terminal.

Jacquard turned to them. "Our flight has been delayed an entire fifteen minutes by our lunch order. Can you believe it?"

"I guess it's hard to get good help these days," said Cody neutrally.

"We have obtained for you a safe location in Monte Carlo." Jacquard checked his watch impatiently. "Parsons informs me you will need equipment, logistical assistance, possibly exfiltration from France. While you are here, may I remind you that you must abide by French law and custom and do nothing that will bring embarrassment to *la Republique*."

"Of course."

A few minutes later, an enlisted man arrived toting two brown paper shopping bags by their handles.

"Ah! *Finalement!* Lunch!" Jacquard raised his eyebrows. "The best we could do was fresh-baked croissants and caviar, eggs with truffle and an assortment of cheeses with a middling grade bottle of Bordeaux. Really, very shoddy for guests. We are normally much better hosts, monsieur."

Cody smiled. "I'm sure we'll manage."

That Jacquard was a tyrant was obvious from his nitpicking and tendency to bully his subordinates. But the man's gruff rudeness concealed a razor-sharp mind and relentless attention to detail. Cody noted how the man relaxed visibly when their plane arrived.

"*ENFIN,*" he grunted. "We can get you onboard and get underway!"

Cody examined the aircraft that taxied onto the apron near the private terminal. The sleek black jet was eighty feet long - the length of a small passenger carrier - and the tips of its wings curled up and back in a sort of cheeky, aerodynamic flourish. Round windows lined the side and two powerful engines nestled at the rear of the fuselage. He recognized the logo of the Dessault aircraft company on the tail wing.

"We are lucky," said Jacquard as he moved them toward the terminal doors. "This is a Falcon 6X, fresh off the assembly line. She is en route for delivery to a millionaire client in Biarritz so I was able to arrange a brief diversion. At top speed, the Falcon flies just shy of Mach 1. You'll be in Monte Carlo shortly."

They crossed the tarmac quickly and were greeted at the doorway by two uniformed flight crew who conducted Cody and company to a dining table in the fore section of the aircraft. Within minutes of their being seated, the warning bell sounded and the Dessault began taxiing into position for take-off. With a final shudder, they lunged down the runway. Despite the power scream of the Pratt & Whitney PW800 turbofans, they were able to hear Jacquard easily as he spoke.

"Parsons filled me in on part of your mission," he said. Noting Cody's look of curiosity, he flashed a sour smile. "Like Horace, I'm retired intelligence. I joined the Directorate as a young man, back when it was still 'la Piscine' - the swimming pool. That was the nickname of the old SDECE because the headquarters was right across the street from the big public swimming pool in Paris. I left a decade ago. But, like Monsieur Parsons, I like to keep my hand in. I settled in Monte Carlo, where I have my business."

They opened the bags and set about attacking Jacquard's 'sub-standard' lunch. It was, in fact, utterly delicious. The croissants were still warm from the oven.

"What can you tell me about Thelma Justice and her presence in town?" Cody asked. "I understand she has a place nearby."

"Ah, yes. Thelma Justice." Jacquard closed his eyes and shook his head. "The women's rights Nazi. She has a large compound about an hour outside of town. There's frequent traffic between that and the local airport. Her organization — the world harmony thing — has a fleet of private jets. They come in and out several times per week. In fact, her company has its own hangar and warehouse at the airport. I've had it under observation before."

"Is she suspected of criminal activity?" Sara asked.

*"Mais, non."* Jacquard made a dismissive, cutting gesture with his hand. "Her people are too careful. They observe every aspect of French law. Thelma Justice has been known to fire employees who even get a traffic ticket. That's how careful she is."

"So why watch her warehouse?" Cody asked.

"Because!" Jacquard exclaimed. "It's almost entirely staffed by Russians!"

# CHAPTER TWENTY-ONE

"THAT'S it for formal meetings today, Mr. President," said the Chief of Staff. "I do have Jared Parnell on ice in my office. His visit here today is unofficial, as you requested."

President Martin Harwood stood up from his chair behind the Resolute desk and stretched. He saw his own image, in shirtsleeves with tie loosened, reflected back at him in the darkened Pella doors of the Oval Office. With his snow-white hair and craggy features, the President looked every moment of his age, but his trim movements revealed the restlessness of his sharp, analytical mind. Outside, night had fallen over DC and most industry and government workers were home or out for the evening. But Harwood, per his habit, was working late, logging in a few more hours before disappearing upstairs to the residence.

"Give me a minute, would you Harry? Then send him in alone."

"Yes, Mr. President."

The Chief of Staff departed through the side door.

Harwood removed his suit jacket from the back of his office chair and pulled it on, tightening his tie and running his fingers through his full white hair. He had requested a briefing from CIA and been disappointed when they sent Parnell. Although firmly stacked and holding at AAD ('almost-assistant-director') level, Parnell was the sort of ruthless climber who mistook bullying for confidence and treachery for competitiveness. President Harwood was a no-nonsense, lead-from-the-front kind of guy. Meetings for him were meant for quick, efficient discussion of information and decision making, not social fencing. He had to be on his toes to edit Parnell's briefings mentally, trimming too self-serving fat from actionable intelligence.

After a brief interval, Parnell entered. The President finished signing a few letters before looking up. "Mr. Parnell. I take it the Director was indisposed?"

"Ah, no sir." Parnell, eyes darting in his narrow face below slicked-back hair, was more nervous than usual. "He asked me to come as the case officer closest to the matter in question."

"Okay." Harwood, already suspicious of the explanation, sat back and steepled his fingers. "So we narrowly stopped Vetrov from delivering a train full of stolen warheads to North Korea. Our intelligence now tells us that he has vanished – dropped off not only our radar but also that of the Russians as well. I assume it's an all-hands-on-deck situation in the FSB right now?"

"Uh, yes sir." Parnell narrowed his eyes. He had not expected the briefing to tilt at this angle. He longed for a puff of his vape pen. "Russian domestic intelligence was the group that alerted the Kremlin to Vetrov's disappearance. Apparently, his driver went to pick him up one morning and he was simply gone."

Harwood grew concerned. That *was* unusual. Generals at Vetrov's level were kept on a short leash. Such men – military officers with service that extended back to the days of the old USSR – were indispensable in the new Russia. Vetrov's disappearance was the sort of loss to ring alarm bells.

"Any word from Jack Cody?" Harwood asked. He noted an immediate change in Parnell at mention of the name – a tightening of the mouth and shoulders, a narrowing of the eyes. The man's dislike for Cody was palpable.

"Nothing from him, Mr. President. Or from Sara Durrell. They've both vanished. Sir, may I be frank?"

"Go ahead." Harwood said tiredly, waving a hand.

"I think it's in our national interest to put as much daylight between ourselves and those two as possible, Mr. President. Vetrov's disappearance is treated as a national crisis because of the clearances he holds and his position in the Russian defense establishment. We can make similar arguments about Cody and Durrell. Those two have clearance, Mr. President. Clearance and information. Information that is no longer under our control now that they're gone."

"What are you saying?"

"Sir, let me cut Cody and Durrell loose and send in our special operations group." Parnell spoke his prepared pitch quickly.

Harwood frowned. Here it was – Parnell's long-awaited power play. The President was aware of Parnell's bureaucratic chicanery, of his fondness for intrigues and theatrics and his deep hatred of Cody and Sara Durrell. Jack and Sara were people of action, not words. Perhaps jealousy on that point was partly why Parnell hated them so much. For months, Parnell had been cultivating his own private constituencies within CIA. Special Operations Group was one. The President was aware that the former head of SOG force and his second-in-command had recently been removed and reassigned at Parnell's request. The men who replaced them were his hand-picked subalterns. Now he was ready to close his fist and effectively control clandestine operations for CIA worldwide.

*Not on my watch,* Harwood thought coolly.

"I appreciate your counsel, Mr. Parnell," said Harwood quietly. "I have no doubt that you have the, ah, good of the Agency topmost in mind. As for now, we're going to hold off on deploying the spec ops group -"

"But sir ..."

"Hang on." Harwood held up a hand. "I have a job for you. I want you to backtrack all known intelligence on Vetrov's whereabouts for the last six weeks. I want to know who he's been seen with, who he's been talking to and whatever you can pick up from ECHELON wiretap intercepts of his cellphone activity. We're going to come at this the long way around. I want this on my desk by tomorrow."

"Yes, sir. And if I may, I -"

"That will be all, Mr. Parnell." Harwood's eye flicked to the red light flashing on his phone console. He interrupted Parnell's next attempt to speak with a cold stare and then waited until the man had left the Oval Office before picking up the phone. "Harwood here," he said.

"I have a call, sir," said the Chief of Staff. "Just came in on the Omega line."

"Put it through." Harwood leaned forward excitedly. The Omega line was a classified, straight-to-the-Oval access telephone number that was in the hands of less than five people worldwide, one of whom was Jack Cody. But it was not his voice that spoke in Harwood's ear.

"Is this President Harwood?" asked a voice in a distinctly British accent.

"Yeah. Who's this?" the President growled.

"Ah, Horace Parsons. Ex MI-6 at your service, sir. I have a message to relay from Jack Cody ..."

# CHAPTER TWENTY-TWO

THE DESSAULT TOUCHED down at a private airfield outside of Monte Carlo, streamers of grime billowing behind it as the plane taxied to a stop. Cody, Sara and Aisha debarked into the hot, gritty afternoon, the dust still settling from the landing. The airfield had the look of a clandestine facility. Cody noted the single runway, made of hard-packed dirt but long enough for jet aircraft to take off and land. There was no terminal building – just a few low-slung offices and a tall fence topped by razor-wire circling the entire installation. Men in unmarked camouflage green walked the perimeter holding machine pistols. From the way they carried themselves, Cody guessed they were Foreign Legion.

"We shall travel in style," announced Jacquard officiously. He led them down the stairway of the Falcon and across the field to a gate beside which stood a guard hut. Another man in unmarked camo, a pistol holstered at his waist, stepped out and conferred briefly with Jacquard before rolling open the gate to the dirt road that ran alongside the fence. A few moments later, a spume of dust heralded the approach of a vehicle.

"Your people?" asked Cody, pointing.

"Taxi," replied Jacquard with a shrug, as if the answer should be obvious.

He was not joking. It soon became clear the driver, an Algerian, had never met Jacquard before. Sara shot Cody an uncertain look, but he shrugged and began packing their luggage into the trunk. Jacquard took the front seat beside the driver and immediately began arguing with him in French.

"A taxi?" whispered Aisha from between them in the back seat. "Is this safe?"

"It actually makes a kind of sense," Cody admitted. "Just another anonymous cab in the streets of town. Hiding in plain sight."

They passed through the rolling, sun-drenched hills of southern France, the dry, heat-scented odor of warm weather plants perfuming the interior. A plume of dust rose in the taxi's wake as they sped along the dirt road. Cody's noticed their tail as they paused to turn onto the main highway.

"We have company," he announced quietly to Jacquard.

The Frenchman's eyes darted to the rear view. Jacquard was pompous, humorless, officious and petty. But he had a keen eye for detail. Like Cody, he could see the dark, narrow shadow closing on them from behind: a single motorcycle, driven by a black-clad rider in a mirrored helmet. It was obvious the man was no casual biker out for a trip through the countryside. Jacquard thumped the taxi driver on the forearm, muttered instructions and then reached for the chicken bar.

"Hold on," he suggested an instant before the driver

downshifted and the taxi leapt forward like a hunting cheetah. Sara and Aisha clutched the edge of their seats as the landscape blurred and the countryside blew past outside.

That the Russians or some other force would have Jacquard's clandestine airfield under observation was no surprise. Cody guessed it was a French intelligence base of some kind – one Jacquard could access as a Backchannel operative. What was surprising was the unexpected skill of their Algerian taxi driver. The man swerved in and around a brace of motorcycles, narrowly missing two before taking the straightaway into town at a breakneck pace. He accomplished all of this, Cody noted, without batting an eye. *Traffic must be insane in Algeria,* he thought.

The taxi rocketed into Monte Carlo. Cody was sure they were likely breaking every speed limit in the country but their Algerian driver flickered from place to place on the roadway with the erratic ease of a butterfly. Sara turned toward the rear window. "Still there," she said crisply. "But he's fallen back about a quarter mile and struggling to keep up."

*"Tres bien!"* Jacquard's voice held real approval. He thumped the taxi driver's arm again, pointed at a street ahead and produced a cellphone. "Get ready to move!" he cried, firing off a quick text.

The taxi shrieked around a corner, drove halfway down an empty block, and squealed to a stop beside an anonymous steel fire door set in a wall between a bookshop and a hair stylist.

*"Vas-y, vas-y!"* cried Jacquard. They leapt from the taxi, grappling their luggage from the trunk. Cody kept one eye on the street corner, expecting the biker as the seconds ticked by. Suddenly, the fire door opened and a

young woman wearing baker's whites and a hair net stood there.

"Inside!" barked Jacquard, tossing the last of the luggage to the sidewalk and thumping the taxi's hood. The Algerian sped off and the four of them poured through the fire door at top speed. The woman in white dragged it shut behind them. A few seconds later, Cody heard the buzz of the pursuer's motorbike pass outside.

"Idiot!" Jacquard crowed. For the first time since they had met him, he smiled. "There is nothing like evading some stupid Russian. Better than sex! Though quite not so good as camembert. Come! *Bienvenue!* Welcome to Boulangerie Jacqard!"

Cody was about to ask why Jacquard was so sure their tail had been Russian. But the question died on his lips as the girl pushed down the crush bar on an inside door and they stepped though into a bakery the likes of which he had never seen.

It was a massive operation, taking up the entire floor of a space the size of a warehouse. Dozens of white-clad bakers and apprentices charged about, some manning huge mixing bowls the size of Volkswagons while others carried trays of finished breads and pastries from the dozens of industrial-strength ovens lining the far walls. Men and women hoisted, tossed, scooped and baked goods at a furious pace. The workspace was, to no one's surprise, loud as a subway platform. But Jacquard's voice was able to cut through the din.

"Michel!" Jaquard waved and one of the white-clad men carrying trays rushed over, proffering the load he bore for inspection. Jacquard bent, squinting at the buns critically before snatching one up, tearing it open to unleash a gust of steam and taking an experimental bite.

He chewed, eyes closed. Then he nodded approval, waving Michel away impatiently.

"Dinner rolls for the grand hotel and casino," he explained, leading them across the floor toward his office. "One cannot be too careful with orders of such importance. The casino's Cordon Bleu is completely insufferable. An absolute *salaud!* Please!" Jacquard held open the door to his office. It was a wide, half-lit space with a low ceiling and a fifty-inch flatscreen on the wall across from the desk. A scattering of open newspapers and magazines covered the couch and coffee table. The din of the bakery vanished the moment Jacquard closed the door behind them.

"How did you know our tail was Russian?" Cody asked.

"Because they are everywhere. Monte Carlo is crawling with Russians these days. Like lice!" Jacquard knocked a pile of magazines from his desk chair and took a seat. "The ones who aren't here on vacation are working in the hotels and casinos. And the criminals, their Bretva, are here to swindle and cheat their way through the gaming tables or run their protection rackets. I know this because I am a brilliant spy. Also because I play cards every Thursday night with the chief of police."

"If there are Russian mafia operating here, then we're in the right place," said Sara. "What about SRV? Is there a Russian intelligence presence in town?"

"No, actually." Jacquard seemed to surprise himself with this news. "There is a certain amount of - how you say? - 'overlap.' Overlap between the Bretva and the spies." He bent and pulled a bottle of red wine from a drawer and poured some into his coffee cup. "But the

SRV and their minions are much more interested in Marseilles and Paris than in the Cote d'Azur."

"Not much for them here of a sensitive nature," Cody said. "Perhaps that's why Vetrov decided to swing his deal here. Little chance of arousing notice from his fellow countrymen."

"One way or the other, you are likely to attract notice in this town." Jacquard stood, coffee cup in hand, and led them to a curtained doorway. "But we here at Boulangerie Jacquard are only too happy to help."

He swept the curtain aside. Cody stepped forward and peered into the room. It was a small storage area crammed with equipment: camouflage uniforms, racks of rifles and small-arms, radio and camera equipment.

"I'll need a tuxedo," Cody said. "I plan to pay a visit to some of the casinos."

Jacquard pushed out his lower lip and made a sweeping gesture with his hand as if such a simple request were a trifle.

"Where will we stay?" asked Sara, looking around the office dubiously.

"Ah." Jacquard's smile was back. "Let me show you."

# CHAPTER TWENTY-THREE

SHE WAS A VISION TO BEHOLD.

Cody stood dockside at the marina, shielding his eyes as he looked up at the superstructure of the *Lorelei*. The name of the cream-colored, three-decker superyacht was emblazoned on the side between the first and second decks in a cool aquamarine font. She looked to be about 180 feet in length and maybe thirty in the beam. She was a fine vessel – the sort that belonged in the hands of some rich playboy to flash as a status trophy. Cody could easily imagine bikini-clad women sunning topless on the foredeck, plotting fun in the sun. But it became clear the moment Jacquard boarded her that *Lorelei* served a different purpose entirely.

The ship was under the watch of a security guard. He and Jacquard conferred quietly for a few minutes before the rent-a-cop gathered up his uniform jacket and lunchbox and departed. Sara and Aisha eyed the luxurious furniture and gleaming fittings with undisguised appreciation. Both beautiful themselves, they recognized a beautiful woman when they met one. Jacquard stepped around them to the sliding glass door of the main lounge and slid it aside. They followed him in.

"A remarkable ship," he muttered. "But, alas, not French. The *Lorelei* is the product of CIA ingenuity. Brought over here last year for operational deployment in Europe, she's found less work than had been anticipated for her. She spends the majority of her time docked here, watched over by yours truly and contract security. Other than admiring glances, she has yet to generate any attention from our Russian adversaries. Just another yacht among yachts. But this? This is no ordinary yacht."

He led them upstairs to the bridge. It was a full wheelhouse after the naval fashion. A series of square reinforced glass windows gave a complete 180-degree view of the waters ahead. Cody stepped forward to inspect the instrument panel. The *Lorelei* was equipped with the latest, greatest nautical gadgets including flatscreen radar and sonar arrays, a Raster navigational system and an engine panel that looked like something from the starship *Enterprise*. A study of its display confirmed for Cody that the yacht had a top speed of 16 knots and a range of around 5,000 nautical miles. This was a ship to bear up under all sorts of weather – the sort to sail an ocean in.

"*Lorelei* was conceived as a floating operational platform for CIA operations in the Mediterranean," Jacquard was saying. "She was designed to interoperate with existing US and NATO naval forces. The six full staterooms aboard have been converted into military-style barracks. If necessary, the *Lorelei* can land a hundred-man strike force anywhere from Gibraltar to Istanbul. Or the coast of Libya, if you prefer. You'll have noticed the satellite array above."

"I didn't," admitted Sara.

"That's because it's hidden." Jacquard grinned sourly. "And the vessel itself is blast-shielded. She can button up and weather the worst kind of storm or even a low-yield nuclear blast. She has stealth capability. And ... this."

Jacquard took the steps down the stairway to the main deck, turned and touched a decorative stud in the paneling. The section of wall slid aside to reveal a hidden compartment. He gestured toward the inside and Aisha moved in to investigate, leaving Cody and Sara to examine it from the doorway.

"You can fit two or three people in here, if you squeeze tight. It's waterproof, so it can also be used as an airlock in the event someone is caught onboard and unable to exit as the ship sinks. There are scuba tanks and masks under the bench there." He pointed. "The ship will be your home during your stay here. No one will bother you."

"So, she is available for our use?"

"If necessary, of course, monsieur. Now you asked about a tuxedo. You'll find one if your size in the closet space of the first stateroom belowdecks."

"You've been very helpful and efficient, Mr. Jacquard."

"It is a genetic quality peculiar to the French, monsieur. I can only take so much credit."

# CHAPTER TWENTY-FOUR

AN HOUR or so after sunset, Cody and Sara sat in a rented Lotus parked on a street in view of the grand Casino Monte Carlo. Dating from the 1850s, the enormous complex with its grand façade and twin bell-style towers had been the backdrop for many great riches-to-rags stories (and, occasionally, their inverse). Even on an off-season night, the glittering edifice was like a palace or cathedral and the foot traffic in and out was brisk. The patronage was toney – wealthy and celebrated people arrived with the air of those expecting to be noticed and paparazzi lurked. It was definitely a place to see and be seen.

Cody sat in the driver's seat, wearing the tuxedo Jacquard had provided. It was surprisingly comfortable. Never one for formal wear, he actually didn't mind the fit. And the jacket came with a few handy extras, one of which was a cleverly concealed, cross-draw shoulder holster. Tucked within was the PAMAS G1, a French version of the Beretta 92 that Jacquard had supplied him with. Cody slipped it out and examined it briefly.

"Nice guns, those 92s," Sara commented. "Like a form-fitting .45 Colt. But I hear the slides tend to break somewhere around the six or seven thousand shot mark."

"I hope I won't be shooting that much tonight," Cody said.

Their eyes met in laughter and held. They were both stone professionals where it came to espionage fieldwork, far too efficient and practical to allow sentiment to cloud their judgment. But there was no doubting that something was growing between them - something that hadn't been there before. They had been in each other's lives for so long as friends and colleagues. Sara had even been best friends with his late wife, Carol. Perhaps for that reason, they had always kept each other at arm's length. But in light of everything they'd shared these past weeks, that had begun to change.

"Cody?"

"Mm?"

"What the hell are we going to do?" She blew out an annoyed sigh and sat back. "If we live through this, what are we going to do about you and me? About us?"

"How do you mean?"

"People like us don't end up with the two-bedroom cottage and the white picket fence. We don't belong there, Cody. Neither of us do. But there's no other way for two people -"

"We'll make a way." Although he spoke softly, he was able to derail her train of thought. "We didn't get here by thinking inside the box, Sara. We are what our lives have made us. And if it's meant to be, we'll find a way to be together. But in order for that to happen, we have to survive this." He shrugged. "I once took an Agency in-service about mortality statistics for field agents and -"

"I took the same one."

"So you know." He pulled on the door handle. "Fortune, as they say, is not in our favor. We have to concentrate on the moment. And the mission."

She nodded. "I'll be right here if you need backup."

"I know." He squeezed her hand. "That's part of why I feel the way I do."

Cody stepped from the Lotus, shutting the bat-wing door behind him. He crossed the darkened street to the main driveway of the Casino Monte Carlo. This was no Walmart. One did not park in front of the façade and obscure the iconic view. Patrons were greeted by parking valets who accepted their keys and parked their cars for them. But this was an expensive prospect, so many patrons chose to walk. Cody fell in amongst the stream of pleasure seekers heading for the main doors.

Stepping inside, Cody noted the high, gold ceilings and magnificent pillars, the glittering chandeliers and massive Turkish rugs of the grand entryway. Security was light, the casino staff with their muted white and black dress code served as eyes and ears for the main crew who, he supposed, were likely upstairs. He caught sight of a uniformed policeman, a holstered black automatic at his waist and the flag of Monaco on his shoulder, so far the only indication Cody had seen of the change in jurisdiction between France and the tiny sea-side principality.

But there was another force present. He could sense it before he saw them – the quiet men in the dark suits, great hulking presences at the bar and standing by the walls. Heavies, and not casino employees. These were the enforcers of the local Russian mob. Not here to collect protection money but instead awaiting debtors to Bretva loan-sharks, men and women driven by desperation to bet what little they had left on one last pitch and toss at the Roulette wheel. Like sharks, these *mefiya* knew the regular haunts of their prey and staged up accordingly. It seemed Jacquard was right. Monte Carlo was thick with Russians.

Little was known about Thelma Justice's personal life. Even her relationship status was a mystery to those who had been following her for years. But it was whispered that she had a weakness for the casino life, enjoyed the odd flutter at the gaming tables. That would put her close to the Russians. And, possibly, Vetrov.

*So where does the Vatican fit into all of this?* he wondered.

Aisha's tablet seemed to be at the center of everything here. Thelma evidently knew of it and had an interest. Possibly the Russians did, too. It wouldn't be the first time the present had been dramatically affected by an artifact from the past. Hitler had sent expeditions in search of both the Holy Grail and Spear of Destiny. Such artifacts had a way of inspiring confidence in the dubious and cementing a cause with legitimacy.

*They also,* Cody thought, eyeing a Russian, *tend to command a very high bidding price.*

It occurred to him that if the Russian *mefiya* was such a heavy presence in the casino then they probably had some inroads to the management. He had to get upstairs, to wherever the offices were. He withdrew back to the main door for a wide-angle view. The bottom floor of the great hall was surrounded by a second-floor balcony. There, he thought, noting a hallway from which two men wearing suits and nametags emerged before taking the stairs down to the main floor. If he could get up there, he could get a sense of how the casino was run and the reach of their security net.

As he lingered, a parcel delivery truck pulled up to the door. Cody watched the driver take off his company ballcap and hang it over the gear shift before disappearing into the back. He re-emerged a second later holding a large package that he ran down to the valet manning the main door. They had a brief exchange in French before the valet led the deliveryman into the casino. For a few precious seconds, there was stillness at the main door.

Cody took two steps across the sidewalk to the delivery truck's door and then took the steps to the cab. He peered through the entryway to the storage bay. As expected, the truck was crammed with parcels. Cody selected a large box and shouldered it before snatching the deliveryman's ballcap and re-entering the casino, headed for the men's room.

Looking inside, he saw it was empty. He stepped into the furthest toilet stall and removed his jacket and bow tie. He hung these from the inside hook, put on the courier company ballcap and shouldered the parcel. Pausing to study himself in the mirror, wearing black pants, a white shirt and ballcap, he resembled a mid-level supervisor. He let himself out, completing the disguise by swiping a clipboard from an unoccupied server's podium and making his way upstairs.

There were more roulette tables and slot machines on the upper level, but Cody was intent on the narrow hallway between the vending machine and the bathroom. He made his way down that way, sweeping his gaze back and forth like a puzzled deliveryman seeking a room. Two employees, a blackjack dealer and a janitor, walked past him without a second glance. The threadbare carpet, bulletin boards with faded notices and glare lighting told him he was definitely entering the employee area.

An open door appeared on his left. He saw a

linoleum-floored break room, complete with fridges and folding furniture. A cluster of casino employees giggled about something at a far table. The next door was an office door marked 'Chef de croupier.' *That would be the floor manager,* Cody thought. He was definitely getting close.

Turning the corner, he came face to face with one of the Russian toughs who was standing in the open doorway of the security office. Behind him, screens glowed with CCTV images of the action down on the floor. Uniformed guards sat monitoring the play, apparently under the control of the second *mefiya* type, who loomed over them.

"Can I help you?" snarled the Russian in the doorway. His French wasn't bad.

"I am looking for the floor manager," Cody replied, masking his poor French behind a make-believe stutter.

The Russian sighed, closed his eyes and pointed back down the hall. Cody thanked him and turned back. He had learned everything he needed to know.

# CHAPTER TWENTY-FIVE

ACROSS TOWN at the Gare Monte Carlo, the 9:25 from Lyon slid into the station along the main track and began to disembark passengers. Because it was a late, off-season train, it was sparsely populated and the platform mostly empty. One man stepped off a passenger car and was greeted as he moved across the platform by a uniformed chauffer.

"*Salaam aleikum*, your highness," said the chauffer quietly. He was, like the man he greeted, Middle Eastern.

"*Aleikum al-Salaam*," replied the passenger. To the casual observer, he was just another well-dressed traveler keeping a low profile. But closer inspection would reveal this was no ordinary traveler. The hands were well-manicured and precise in their movements. The expensive gold watch tastefully accented with precious stones, the scrupulously coiffed goatee, the expensive cut of the clothes revealed him as a man of substance. The careful tailoring of his suit jacket concealed the high-calibre automatic holstered there. Close inspection revealed this to be a very dangerous man, indeed.

The Prince Achmed bint al-Ahmad moved with the economy of an apex predator. For that is what his father had bred him to become – a wolf among dogs. Theirs was a royal house that could trace its lineage back to the time of the Prophet. And Achmed, as was fitting for an eldest son of House al-Ahmad, was occupied with protecting the family name and increasing its fortunes. His mission in Monte Carlo fell firmly in the first category. It was a painful duty he bore stoically. They approached a Lincoln parked at the deserted sidewalk outside the station.

"Any more on the whereabouts of the man, Cody?"

The chauffer held open the rear door. "The sighting is not yet confirmed, your highness ..."

"I know," snapped the prince. He took a seat and immediately drew a cellphone from his pocket. He had come here on a tip, more of a slim hunch. The sheikh had sent his oldest son to collect his sister, Aisha, and a few days ago he had had her in hand. Their father was an indulgent man but his patience had limits. It was one thing for his sister to study ancient historical riddles in libraries and at the feet of university professors. It was quite another for her to venture off and play fast and loose with her safety and the family honor by pretending to become Indiana Jones.

*She has cost our family a great deal of disgrace,* he thought, thumbing up his quick dial list. His call was answered on the first ring.

"*Salaam,* my prince."

"*Salaam,* Ali Yusuf. What is your update for me?"

"My prince, still no sign of the Princess Aisha. But reports of a man matching Cody's description have circulated among the Russian underworld here in town.

We now have a picture taken at the casino by one of our operatives."

"Send it at once." Achmed hung up. A moment later, his cell beeped with an incoming text. He opened the message.

There.

He held in his hands the image of the man who had taken Aisha from him, who had broken into his waterfront refuge in America, overcome his guards and made off with his sister, the Princess. The disgrace upon their family was one thing, but the personal disgrace he as eldest son now faced was horrific. The man named Cody had overturned all his plans and once again placed their family in danger.

For the last time.

Now they had a lead on him. The picture also gave them a place and time from which to commence looking. They would track down Aisha. And if grabbing her meant punishing Cody, then so be it. He would be successful.

It was just a matter of time.

# CHAPTER TWENTY-SIX

"THERE YOU GO," said Jacquard, climbing into the passenger side of the Citroen and handing Cody the binoculars. "This is the only vantage from which one can look down on the compound."

"It's a nice spot," Cody admitted. That Jacquard's contacts in the city planning office were good enough turn up directions to an unfinished road-works project high in the mountains was impressive.

"Ms. Justice and her staff of militant lesbian Amazons value their privacy. There's even a helicopter that patrols. Although not in this weather." The Frenchman cast a wary gaze up at the forbidding vault of grey clouds. "I don't think a personal reconnaissance is worthwhile, monsieur. If you can just give me 24 hours, I can get my hands on a mini drone unit with a good camera. You'll save yourself a great deal of time and energy. To say nothing of risk."

Cody did not reply. He had learned that offering an alternative point of view – any alternative – provided Jacquard with an opportunity to do what he loved most, which was to argue. Cody didn't have time for that now. None of them did. Vetrov was in the midst of setting up a new deal with WMDs. Right now what Cody needed was answers, not options. And he was going to get them by any means possible.

He lifted the binoculars and began glassing the compound.

For an organization dedicated to the values of 'world harmony', Thelma Justice's "order" had a distinctly military edge to it. The compound below reminded Cody of the US army installations he had visited in forward areas around the world. Fenced in, gated and patrolled regularly, it was a place that telegraphed its secure status as a warning to the world. He had already encountered the Furies security detail once before. Now here they were out in numbers, patrolling the pathways between the compound's buildings. A dozen or so Quonset huts were clustered in the rear, obviously used as storage and barracks for the crew. Personnel moved on foot or navigated around on ATVs. Cody noted the ATV drivers all wore overcoats and mirrored helmets.

"I think I have a way to get inside," he said. "Can we verify the fence is unmonitored?"

With a frustrated sigh, Jacquard dug through a leather equipment satchel until he found a small black box. Leads spring from the side, ending in clamps. Then he clamped his cap on his head and gestured for Cody to lead on.

They took a footpath descending from the roadworks into the stone teeth of the valley below. This was no pretty Alpine trail. The way underfoot was treacherous, with sections of gravel and sliding shale. More often than not they were hemmed in by claustrophobic fangs of rock that shot skyward, sometimes even leaning in to block out the light. But eventually they came down within trees and, a few hundred yards further on, the fence of the compound.

Jacquard put the clamps to the fence and hit a switch on the side of the black box. One at a time, three rectangular lights lit up: two green, one yellow. He switched off the box and retrieved the clamps.

"Electrified but not at the moment. Probably switched on after dark. But not wired. Not monitored," said Jacquard.

"I'll cut my way in," Cody said, removing a multi-tool from his belt. "You go park down the road from the front gate. I won't be long."

"Good luck, monsieur," Jacquard said quietly. Then he retreated through the trees to the footpath. Cody got to work.

# CHAPTER TWENTY-SEVEN

HE CUT a triangular section of fencing close to the ground, lifted it and shimmied under on his back. Once inside, he folded the section back down and secured it with a zip-tie. He would not need it again.

Cody was behind a Quonset hut. There were four of them in this section of the compound, connected by roadways to the other buildings on the property. From where he was, Cody could see a multi-story office complex outfitted with an array of satellite and internet communications equipment that would have looked at home on any embassy rooftop. Thelma Justice and her Order of World Harmony came well-equipped.

He stayed put, monitoring the area for a full minute. He could hear voices and the purr of ATV motors but knew immediately he was in a remote sector of the compound. This place was patrolled but was not a priority. *Storage,* he thought. There was no better place to start. After an ATV buzzed past, he crept to the front of the nearest Quonset hut and peered around the corner.

He was on a dusty street of the things, the dirt in the road marred by tracks of recent passage.

He tried the flimsy wooden door at the front of the hut and was not surprised to find it unlocked. Easing it open, he slipped into the dark room and shut it behind him. His fingers found a light switch.

The Quonset hut was not particularly large. But emptied of furniture it could hold a great deal. And this one held stacks of merchandise on shrink-wrapped pallets. All the same thing by the looks of them. He stepped forward and stripped the plastic from one pallet load and examined the contents. The pallet held First Aid kits, perhaps as many as four hundred identical such items zipped into their little canvas pouches. Cody estimated the force here in the compound at maybe a hundred. Making a quick calculation, he estimated that if the goal was to give one to each person on site, they had roughly 1400 too many.

He tucked the plastic back around the stacked palette, switched off the light and snuck out to the next Quonset hut.

He closed the door behind him. No need to switch on the light as the bulb was already burning. There, hung from racks like hangars in a dry cleaner's shop, were rows of clothing. In this case, all identical. Cody shivered when he recognized them.

*Radiation suits.*

It was impossible to say how many were hung there exactly, but he counted one hundred just within the first few feet of the nearest rack. Given the number and length of racks in the room, the mind boggled at the mathematics ...

"Hey! You!"

The woman who stepped from the back room was

not a Fury. Instead of a military uniform, she wore a white smock, like a lab worker. Seeing Cody, she dropped the clipboard in her hands and fumbled for her pocket. Two giant steps and Cody was there beside her, a fist wrapped around the wrist holding a cellphone.

"Relax," he said quietly. "I'm not going to hurt you."

"Get *OUT!*" Her voice, although a hoarse whisper, was urgent and shot through with fear. "You can't be here! They'll kill us!"

"Kill us?" Cody took the phone from her hand and stepped to the nearest rack. "Over these... biohazard suits? What's so special about...?"

He peeled back the collar of one to look at the label there.

## CERBERUS

AND THEN SUDDENLY THE woman was moving, diving for the back room. There must have been some sort of alarm panel back there because suddenly a claxon shrieked and a red light began swirling outside the Quonset hut. By the time Cody followed her into the room, she was gone, the back door open. Voices rose from the front:

"In here! Check the back!"

Cody heard the sound of the Furies as they crashed through the front door. Cody bolted out the back, and straight into one rounding the corner on an ATV. He lowered his head and shoulder-checked her off the bike. The woman flew from the saddle, hitting the ground with a crash as Cody leapt onto the ATV and gunned the throttle.

"There!" One of the Furies came through the back door, hand clawing at her holster.

Cody spun the wheel and sped away. Although not built for the racing circuit, the ATV was a speedy little beast. He thundered down the straightaway, past a trio of Furies that were unloading a truck at another Quonset hut. At a yell from one, they dropped what they were doing and moved to block him. Cody jerked the wheel, leaned left, then right and poured on the gas. He made it through, clipping one on the way by.

He turned off the dirt track between Quonset huts and found himself on a paved road. A pair of ATVs were hurtling toward him, a Fury astride each one. Seeing Cody, they shared a signal and then peeled in opposite directions in a practiced pit maneuver. He slowed, knowing it gained him distance. The Furies were each taking a shoulder of the road, ready to come in and pincer him. Cody twisted the handlebars of his ATV to the left, right into the nose of the oncoming ATV.

FOR A SECOND, the Fury wasn't sure what to do. Cody poured on the speed, counting on her to veer at the last moment, which she did – right into her partner. In place of a grand explosion come the dull thud of two bodies striking one another and the groan of the one that hit the ground first. Their ATVs tangled and spun into a ditch and Cody motored on.

A woman ran out of the doorway of a nearby build-ing, hands scrambling frantically over the frame of an assault rifle. It looked to Cody like the slide on her assault rifle had jammed. That's how it appeared anyway, in the instant before he shot her down. She fell in a twisted heap on the sidewalk.

He saw the gate up ahead, and the sentry struggling to draw it closed. He drew the G1 from its holster and scared the sentry back into the guardhouse with two shots. Then he sped out the gate and onto the street. And there was Jacquard's car parked ahead!

Cody leapt from the ATV and sprinted for the passenger door. He caught sight of Jacquard's startled expression in the rear-view mirror as the first of the Furies poured out of the compound, rifles raised.

"Get ready to punch it!" Cody cried.

Jacquard fired up the engine. The first bullets tore up the street from Thelma Justice's private militia. Cody grasped the door handle, pulled and dove into the Citroen. Jacquard didn't even wait for the door to close. A second later, they were racing up the street like the very Devil himself was in pursuit of them.

# CHAPTER TWENTY-EIGHT

IN THE HOT, dusty country on the French side, the historic Medieval church of St. Nazaire sits brooding among the dry rolling hills that march to the border with Monaco. The church itself was closed shortly after Vatican II, when the aging clergy and congregation dwindled away. Despite its historic heritage, the place was too remote to draw tourists. And so it had remained shuttered – seemingly abandoned and forgotten by the march of progress. But in truth, St. Nazaire was far from forgotten. And watchful eyes monitored its grounds from hidden blinds day and night.

Under the moonlight, a truck approaching through the scrub drew the attention of the observers. Beneath the heavy moon, it blew up dust in its wake, jouncing over the rutted road. It turned into the curved driveway before the abandoned church and slowed. The church doors opened and a group of fifteen men debarked, all dressed in black. Within seconds they had vanished into the church, pulling the doors closed behind them. The truck turned and drove back the way it came. Within a minute, silence and stillness had returned to St. Nazaire, the interruption noted only by the hidden sentries who resumed their watchful duty.

Inside the church, Father Valachi of the Order of St. Adrian counted his men. When he was sure they were all accounted for, he turned to the aged priest who had held open the doors for them.

"Thank you, Father deVilliers. Has the Cardinal briefed you?"

"He has, Father Valachi. I have arranged for your men to be quartered in the church hall and have obtained three rental vehicles, anonymous black Peugeot 308s. The armory is ready for your review."

"Excellent." Valachi turned to Turnois, his lieutenant. "Get the men settled then join us in the armory."

"Yes, father." Turnois, one of the Dominican brothers under Valachi's leadership and an ex-Foreign Legionnaire, got the men moving while Valachi followed deVilliers through a doorway into a storage area. Racks of automatic weapons lined both walls. Shelves and tables held maps, optical and tactical equipment. Valachi stepped to the nearest table as deVilliers turned on the lights and bent to examine some night vision gear.

"ENVG Systems. The same ones used by American special forces," said deVilliers. "There are enough for your entire team. Assuming you may choose to operate at night."

"That may be very necessary. Have your operatives located any sign of the princess?"

"No. But we have a good CCTV photo of Cody at the casino earlier tonight. We know he is in Monte Carlo or staying somewhere nearby." deVilliers produced an envelope from his cassock. "And a package arrived by courier from Saint Theresa's."

Valachi opened the envelope and scanned the contents. As usual, the sisters running the analysis and cryptographic arm of the Black Cardinal's operation had come through for them. Contained within were fifteen false passports and matching driver's licenses for Valachi and his men. In a separate envelope were the keys for the 308s. Turnois arrived as Valachi finished putting the items back in the envelopes.

"If there is nothing else you require of me, I shall attend to dinner for your men," said Father deVilliers.

"Thank you, father."

They watched the old priest depart and waited for the door to close behind him before speaking.

"The nuns have been busy on our behalf." Valachi handed Tournier the envelope of passports. "These are of excellent quality. See that those are distributed. Arm the men and then set up watches for the night. We're going to take a drive in one of the cars Father deVilliers has provided for us. I want to take a look at the casino."

"Very good, father."

"And tell Vincent to set up his laptop. I may have a hacking job for him."

"Right away, father."

After Tournois left to make arrangements, Valachi went to the door of the church and stepped outside. The night air was cool as he lit a cigarette and considered his options.

The after-action report he had received confirmed Cody had taken the princess from her brother Achmed. Whether the girl had gone willingly or not was of little importance. Valachi was focused on the fragment and returning it to Vatican control. He was intent on that and little else. But he admitted to himself that the tablet and what it signified made him uneasy.

Princess Aisha's fascination with the false prophet Thelma Justice suggested feminist sympathies. For his part, Father Valachi thought the feminist revolution and consequent imposition of women's ways into society had gone too far. Some denominations even had women in positions of religious leadership. A few even worshipped a female god...

The coincidence of the tablet being in the possession of the Princess who was now close to Thelma Justice was no idle matter in Valachi's mind. He knew such items as the tablet could become the foundation of schisms, of entire religious movements. Imagine a power-hungry woman in possession of a Biblical fragment that questions our entire understanding of relationships between the genders.

Now imagine that woman in charge of a global organization that was well armed and well funded.

That such events could be of danger to the church was obvious. But this went even further. Such a turn of events posed a challenge to the entire social order. In the ensuing chaos, millions could die. It occurred to Valachi that he was one of a very few men in the world with the capability to put a stop to it.

He checked his watch. They were behind schedule.

# CHAPTER TWENTY-NINE

WHAT THELMA JUSTICE loved most about sexing Greb Vetrov was not the great languorous shuddering release he ignited in her (although that was sweet). It was not the sensation of satisfaction when she saw his face contort in joy. It was not even the money or the resources their union represented. All of these things were sweet, but they were in no way what she loved most about their sex.

It was the *power*.

To be sure, Greb Vetrov was a Russian flag officer. But underneath, he was a snarling, covetous, aggressive, competitive animal. When he was atop her, she often imagined him ravishing another woman. Or attacking her. Because there was little difference in the way a man like him fought and the way he made love. Both circumstances were ones in which his power, released in a nova of heated violence, filled the room. It was that kind of power she longed to wield herself.

And now Greb Vetrov had made that possible.

The limousine passed through the darkened streets at

2 in the morning. The restaurants were closed, the stores shuttered and the café tables pulled back from the sidewalks. From the backseat snuggled beside Vetrov, she could look out at the cold empty streets and closed curtains behind which power slept. Sleeping power was no better than power wasted. Thelma's appetite for power was as ravenous as her appetite for food or sex. She studied on it, fantasized and wondered about it, obsessed over it day and night. Under the microscope of her intellect, not one single atom of it would go wasted.

The car sidled up to the silent docks. An old tugboat sat moored at the pier, its dark iron front rusting. The name *Matilda* was painted on its wheelhouse in faded white script. A single deck lamp burned dull yellow on the bridge.

"Come," said Vetrov. He let himself out, drawing Thelma with him. They crossed the silent dock to the tug's deck rail and stepped aboard. To say the tug was in poor repair would be an understatement. Equipment lay scattered across its deck. The paint was peeling and water pooled in open spaces.

"Nice boat," she remarked, stepping over a fallen bucket.

"*Matilda* is crap. Never get a second glance." Vetrov cross to the cabin door and fitted a key into the lock. "Nobody ever notice her. Nobody."

He opened the door and led them down a steel stairway to a lit hold belowdecks.

Reaching the foot of the ladder he turned. "Before you see it, you must tell me something," he said quietly.

She paused one step from the bottom, surprised. It was not his way to talk, or to show any kind of need or vulnerability. But here he was exposing himself – opening up about his need to know her motivations.

"What will you do with ultimate power?" He raised his hands from his sides and let them drop. "This is everything, no? The kind of power that purchases you a seat at the table. You are in love with influence and you are in love with power. Also in love with me. I am about to give you key to great power. Which door will you open?"

At this, she smiled. "I had never thought about it that way before," she admitted. "But opening doors is a good way to think about it. For that is what I intend to do, with the keys you have provided."

"These keys, when used, open doors to whole new ages."

"I remember." She recalled the images she had seen of flattened buildings, skylines smeared black and skeletal domes stripped of tile. "Greb, who must rule?"

"The strong."

"Always. But the strong grow corrupt." She moved down toward him, taking him in her arms and gazing lovingly into his eyes. "Ever notice how the same cycle of civilization repeats over and over again? Good times bring decadence. With decadence comes corruption. After that, the fall and men must work hard again to regain the good times."

"Men ... destroy." He shrugged again. "Is part of how we create. Lion eats cubs lioness has with former sire. Is same with men. First we must destroy what other men create. Then we build."

"And how many die?"

Again, the dismissive wave of the hand. This time he said nothing. He didn't have to.

"What if there was a different way?" she asked. "A way forward without so much destruction and death? No, wait! Listen to me! It can be done. What must be proven is our will. Our will must be perfect. It must be beyond question. We must love what we want to save so much that we are willing to destroy it."

*Love what we want to save so much we must be willing to destroy it...*

A strange feeling sang in Greb Vetrov's chest. It was a sinister, alien thing – a kind of crawling tingle that embraced the frames of his lungs before shuddering and causing his mind to tilt. From this perspective, her words made a strange kind of sense.

"You have ... this way?"

"I have ... a way." She touched his arm. "A way out of the cycle."

"Is impossible! Is cycle of history."

"Yet how many lives lost?"

"What matters is power."

"Exactly. And to achieve power, one must disrupt the cycles of power. To make history, one must disrupt the cycles of history."

"And you plan to do this? How?"

She kissed him. "Show me," she whispered.

He turned and stepped to a closed hatch. Tapping in a numeric code on the keypad, he pulled on the wheel and revealed a steel and concrete storage hold. It was scoured clean and empty, save for racks of identical steel suitcases. Slightly larger than your ordinary executive briefcase, each one was burnished clean, sturdy but nevertheless lightweight and portable. Each one, Thelma noted, came with a combination dial.

Vetrov stepped over to the nearest case, pulled it down from the rack and opened it across a table near the front by the hatch.

"Latest achievement in Russian nuclear science. Miniaturization. See the steel plate? Is forced recombination chamber. Nuclear detonator. These plastic rectangles hold the yield charge. These units are called 'Hummingbirds.' Each one is ten times more power than the bomb that destroyed Hiroshima."

"And you've brought me how many?"

"Thirty."

"That will be enough."

"To do what?"

"To break the cycle of history." She smiled.

VALACHI FOUND the door to the security office. It was partly open, showing two uniformed guards inside monitoring the action on the casino floor via CCTV. Down the hall was a fire door leading to a flight of stairs.

*Perfect,* he thought. He placed himself there and waited.

The girl appeared at the head of the stairs a minute or two later. She had obviously been to the washroom and freshened up. She carried herself with a brisk, powerful sort of purpose, her clutch under an arm, mouth curled in a smirk of amusement.

"Well hello, monsignor," she purred. "How are you this night?"

"Feeling quite amorous," he said huskily. "Come."

He pushed on the crush bar and led her through the emergency door and out onto the cement landing. The door closed behind them. One minute later, it opened and Valachi emerged alone.

Turnois came to the top of the stairs. Put his hand in his pocket. Nodded once.

Valachi sprinted down the hall to the security office. "Please! Come help! There's a young woman who has fallen in the stairwell!"

Instantly, both guards were up and moving quickly. Valachi led them down the hall to the fire door and out onto the landing. Turnois took that opportunity to slip past them and into the security office.

He examined the CCTV monitors, peered under the desks and found the hard drives. Reaching into his pocket, he produced a small disk about the size of a quarter fashioned from some kind of black polymer. He squeezed it once and a red pin-point light winked on. Reaching behind a hard drive, he clipped the magnetized

# CHAPTER THIRTY

"So OUR CIA operative infiltrated this pleasure palace." Father Valachi, standing on the sidewalk beside his lieutenant, Turnois, examined the façade of the Grand Casino. "What do you suppose he was looking for?"

"Not Muslims, to be sure," quipped Turnois. "They don't drink. Or gamble."

Valachi chuckled. "Some do. Just as there as some Catholics who occasionally sneak off to attend Anglican services with a friend. But our princess is not such a one. No, if our man was here then he was searching for something. The question is what."

"Some CCTV footage might be helpful," offered Turnois, noting the cameras mounted on the exterior of the building.

"My thoughts exactly." Valachi smiled. "How long will you need to place your device?"

"Moments," Turnois assured his superior. "If I can gain access to their CCTV system room, I can clip the RF tracker to the back of a hard-drive. A minute or two. That's all I shall require."

"Then you shall have it, my friend." Valachi looked both ways and began crossing the street. "Let's go."

They gained the entrance, smiling to the fawning security staff, playing the part of two country bumpkin priests in town to lose a little money. They strolled to the bar and ordered drinks – a Perrier water for Valachi, a Coke for Turnois. Their drinks arrived and they turned their backs to the bar as one to scan the room. There was plenty of action at the gaming tables, although it was early afternoon. Even a few of Monte Carlo's more ambitious prostitutes were up early and working the clientele.

"I don't think she'll be bothering us," muttered Turnois as one sauntered by without giving them even the slightest acknowledgement.

"It's a perk of our profession." Valachi sipped his mineral water. "We avoid unnecessary entanglements with the fairer sex. But in this case, I believe their assistance could prove a boon."

"Oh?"

"Indeed." Valachi nodded toward a slim-hipped, dark-haired young thing who was lounging at the end of the bar. "If we are making a disaster movie, Father Turnois, I would cast her as the perfect victim. You catch my meaning?"

"Of course, father."

"Ah – let us say … *monsignor* for this little drama. Tell her to meet me on the second floor. I assume that's where their security office will be …"

"Most likely yes, fa – Ah, *monsignor.*"

"Go thou and attend to the Lord's work, Father Turnois." Valachi toasted his subaltern and watched him depart.

Turnois approached the young prostitute at the end of the bar. She was different from the others, who tended to float around in packs of two or three. T[...] alone, drinking confidently by herself, eye[...] clients of quality. This one was a discerning n[...] Turnois realized. He acted accordingly. Casting [...] cally worried glance over his shoulder at Vala[...] approached shyly.

"Good evening, miss. How are you?"

The young hooker turned, took one look at Tu[...] collar and hoisted an eyebrow. "Really?" she asked.

Turnois chuckled. "Alas, no. My tastes ar[...] different in that regard. No, I am here on behalf [...] someone…"

"Your friend over there? The one with the scarre[...] face?" She flicked her chin. "You two aren't queer for[...] each other? Because I can do threesomes, but that costs extra."

"That gentleman happens to be a monsignor of the Catholic Church. He is very highly placed in the Curia. And he has a great deal of money."

At the mention of money, her interest sharpened noticeably. Down at the other end of the bar, Valachi finished his drink and made for the stairs.

"The monsignor would like to meet you discreetly on the second floor. It's a thousand dollars US just to show up. Everything afterwards is an extra for which you will be compensated."

The girl watched Valachi disappear up the staircase. "Let me go freshen up," she said quietly and disappeared into the bathroom. Turnois smiled. He had her hook, line and sinker.

device to the back. Then he was up and out of the room, heading back down the corridor.

"Father, what happened?" he asked theatrically as Valachi and the two guards returned from the stairwell.

"It's the most tragic thing. So young. I cannot be certain, but it seems she fell down the steps and broke her neck, poor thing."

"Merciful God…"

"Indeed, Father Turnois." Valachi patted his friend's arm. "God's mercy is what this is all about."

# CHAPTER THIRTY-ONE

*SO IT ALL comes down to this,* thought Cody.

He sat alone in the secure documents room. Cody looked around the walnut paneled chamber. It was a small space - just large enough for a sumptuous rug, mahogany table and chair. The shelves held all manner of rare volumes and the rack of steel drawers along the opposite wall held safety deposit boxes. A file lay on the table before him. Jacquard and the priest administering the archives had just left, closing the door behind them, locking Cody in with this single English typewritten copy of a study on the tablet commissioned by the Archbishop of Avignon in 1939.

*Who is the Archbishop to order a study into so sacred a relic?* Cody had asked.

*The Archbishop of Avignon was once the Pope,* replied Jacquard, as if that were obvious. *Note the year. 1939. One year before the Nazis took France.*

*What happened then?*

*This,* Jacquard had patted the manuscript, *went underground.*

There was a card clipped to the front of the file tracking the dates it was accessed and read. Cody noted the last viewing had taken place in April of 1978. Then he turned his attention to the title page.

## AN INQUIRY CONCERNING THE TEMPLAR KNIGHTS & THE MARIAN FRAGMENT: RITUAL, HERESY & LEGACY

Something about the tablet now in Aisha's possession had consumed the Templars. According to Aisha, it caused them to completely change the way they worshipped and lived. Ultimately, this led to their persecution by the Pope and the elimination of their order. What Cody now held was the only known study of why – and exactly what – had happened. History wasn't normally his big area of interest, but the fact that the Church had seen fit to conceal this knowledge from the Nazis made it all the more fascinating. The Church had investigated and generated two identical reports, one in French and one in English. Both resided in this archive. Cody began reading the latter.

The document outlined some background information about the community known as the Desert Rabbis. They reminded Cody of the Taliban and some of the other religious extremists he had encountered, although these guys didn't seem terribly violent. These were not Zealots – just deeply religious men who wanted to be left alone. So far as he could tell, they just wanted to live apart from what they saw as the 'pollution' of Roman culture. All well and good. Until the day Jesus arrived.

Cody knew there were so-called apocryphal and gnostic Gospels – versions of the Jesus story that had been disqualified from inclusion in the Bible by learned doctors of the church. Cody had read a couple once just out of curiosity and been struck by how obviously fake some of the stories sounded. But the record kept by the Desert Rabbis struck a different tone.

> "... came to pass the rabbi from Galilee, known to his people as Yeshua, came to seek refuge among us for a time. On the second feast day, he opened his mouth and taught us of the first Book of Moses, speaking of the creation of woman. The rabbi spoke at length about the miracle of woman, how the Lord so loved woman that He entrusted her with the gift of issuing forth life. But Rabbi Yeshua then spoke of how with this sanction to give life came also a [lacunae - possibly 'intimacy'?] with death."

Cody raised his eyebrows at that. And read on.

There was more to the sermon. Cody couldn't follow it entirely but knew enough about mysticism to recognize references to the Kabbalah, or Hebrew system of ceremonial magic. That sort of thing was strictly a no-no with the organized church. So, it made sense the Vatican would keep a wrap on this stuff. That's when things got really weird.

> "And the Rabbi Yeshua spoke of his twin, Judith, and her ministry in the Kingdom of Tyre. He spoke of her friendship with Mary and Martha and her part in the resurrection of Lazarus ... of how God perfected her both in the sanction to give life and the [lacunae - possibly 'intimacy'?] with death."

It took Cody a minute or two to recognize that he

was no longer breathing. He looked away from the page, drew a deep lungful of air and continued reading.

> *"The Heresy of Judith, the unrecognized twin of The Savior, died under the hammer of St. Paul."* [the report continued] *"It enjoyed a brief renaissance in Persia under the Ismaili chieftain Hassan i-Sabbah before being driven underground and rediscovered by the Templars. It began with their recovery of the Marian Fragment during their occupation of the Temple Mount during the Crusades."*

So the Crusaders took up the Doctrine of the Twin Saviors, Jesus and Judith ...

It was mind-blowing.

The paper continued to lay it out from there. The basic argument: that the Christ was incomplete without its twin aspects of Jesus and Judith. That only the power of the two conjoined could achieve resurrection (as in the cases of Lazarus and the daughter of Jairus). And so the Templars, in recognition of this fundamental truth...

... had allowed women to become Templars.

Cody hunched over the page, reading quickly now.

> *"Beginning during the leadership of Baldwin, sergeant of the Temple guard, the first women at arms joined the Templars. They were accounted present in the rolls of the brothers at arms and were given position in the flank wings of Templar actions. The female Templars, virgins all, acquitted themselves with unique gallantry and were accorded recognition among the Temple leadership."*

And so there had been women Templars.

And Aisha, in possession of this fragment and knowledge, had attempted to contact Thelma Justice.

Cody stood, closing the manuscript and pushing the chair into the table. He stepped out into the hallway, where Jacquard was busy arguing with the priest. Seeing Cody was done, he spat one final insult before moving toward the exit. They made their way out to the car.

"You found what you needed to know?" the Frenchman asked.

"Yes. It's all quite clear to me now."

"*Bien,*" Jacquard grunted, starting up the car. "Good thing my brother-in-law manages the archives."

# CHAPTER THIRTY-TWO

"OUR BREAKTHROUGH WAS UNEXPECTED," admitted Turnois. He kept his voice low, audible to himself and Father Valachi but not to any of the other pedestrians sharing the sidewalk with them. They walked side by side, heads bent in confidential conversation. Their clerical collars generated some attention – and the occasional smile – from passersby.

*Typical response,* thought Valachi. In western Europe, Catholic priests are ubiquitous enough that he and his team were able to hide in plain sight.

"How did it come about, this breakthrough?"

"It seems one of CIA's operatives had a sudden crisis of faith." Turnois paused at a crosswalk, Valachi doing likewise as traffic passed. Up ahead was the marina. "He was stationed in Poland. He made the abrupt decision to leave the CIA and renounce his citizenship. But instead of going to China or Russia, he came to us. Presented himself to the Papal nuncio and requested sanctuary. He is in the Vatican now."

"Very convenient!" enthused Valachi.

The signal turned and Turnois led the way across the street. "Of course, the United States is aware of the situation. They have lodged a formal complaint through their ambassador to the Holy See. But there is nothing they can do. Meanwhile, our friend has been receiving regular visits from Cardinal D'Agostino's envoys. He has been given the code designation 'Songbird.'"

"Very poetic. And apropos."

They were approaching the docks, now, a forest of masts, antennae and radar arrays filling the sky. Turnois brought them to a point opposite the traffic entrance to the pier and turned to face the large window of a boutique specializing in bedding. Valachi did likewise, appreciating the unobstructed view of the docks reflected in the glass.

"According to Songbird, CIA operations in Europe have proceeded apace, quickening with the advent of Brexit. But some sectors have been more active than others. Germany and England in particular. Most of their operations in France are confined to the larger metropolitan areas. There is not much for them to do here…"

"So their safehouses are unoccupied, unused." Valachi nodded. "The perfect locale for someone like Cody to secret himself and his confederates."

"There are safehouses," replied Turnois. "And there are safe… *boats.*" He gestured toward the window, as though pointing out a product when he was in fact motioning at the reflection of a boat. "That one. There."

Valachi considered the reflection and then turned, disguising the movement with a stretch. The ship lay directly across from them, a long white yacht. Although not a nautical man, Valachi recognized a superior feat of engineering when he saw one. Yes, it was a lovely ship.

He studied the name on the side before turning back to the window.

"The *Lorelei.*" He rolled the name on his tongue. "And what has our friend Songbird revealed about the ship?"

"Intended to function as a base for clandestine operations in the Mediterranean. The ship itself is equipped with state-of-the-art surveillance and data gathering technology. Capable of carrying equipment and personnel, she was constructed at considerable cost."

"And?"

"For the past year, she has been moored here. Doing precisely nothing."

"So *Lorelei* is a prime candidate for use by agents on the run. Like our erstwhile Mr. Cody. Come." He touched Turnois' shoulder. "Let us take a closer look."

They crossed the street. A trio of nuns spotted them in the crosswalk and bowed their heads. Valachi smiled and gave them his blessing, shrugging to ensure the movement of his arm did not reveal the automatic holstered under his left armpit. They gained the opposite curb and approached the entrance to the marina.

"The yacht itself sees almost no activity whatsoever," said Turnois. "It appears that our CIA friends have engaged a private security firm to have a guard onboard twenty-four hours per day."

"And this guard? He's vigilant?"

Turnois grinned. "He's a rent-a-cop, father. He does one lazy patrol above-decks every hour or so. Can't be bothered to stir from his chair more frequently than that."

"Small mercies." Valachi grinned back. "Has the guard's routine varied at all in the past twenty-four hours?"

"It has, father. Our surveillance indicates the guard was sent home recently. Apparently, the service has been held in abeyance until further notice."

"It would seem to indicate the vessel is in use."

"My thoughts exactly, father."

They strolled along the pier, their appearance as tourists reinforced by their leisurely gait and the large camera strapped around Turnois' neck.

"I think some photographs of the sea are in order," sniffed Valachi.

"Oh, agreed." Turnois held up the camera. "Perhaps you would care to stand over there, father?"

Valachi walked down to the edge of the pier and turned with his back to the sea. He clasped his arms behind his back and smiled as if posing for a picture. Aiming the camera in his direction, Turnois cheated the angle until his superior was crowded into the further corner of the frame. The majority of the fish-eye lenses' view was consumed by the *Lorelei*. A dock official wandered by as they were finishing up.

"Bonjour, fathers." The dock worker, an elderly Frenchman, doffed his cloth cap to the men. "So nice to see priests here! I normally only ever see you on Sunday at church."

"We're so glad you attend church," replied Valachi. "I would imagine a man in your profession must be quite busy."

"Busy enough." The dock worker shrugged, indicating the nearby ships with a flick of his clipboard. "Checking the docking registrations of our tenants. The arrangement changes everyday. Some stay. Some leave."

"What about this one?" Turnois asked, indicating *Lorelei*. "Such a fine boat! I can't imagine she'll remain moored here long…"

"This one?" The dock worker spat. "Useless. Sits here day after day. The only one who ever comes by is the baker, Jacquard. I think he is the owner. Or part-owner, anyway. He comes to chat with the security guard from time to time."

"That's very interesting," said Father Valachi, and smiled.

# CHAPTER THIRTY-THREE

ALONE BEHIND THE wheel of a Maserati, Prince Achmed bint al-Ahmad scanned the sidewalks for any sign of his sister. He was far too sophisticated an operator to rely on personal reconnaissance alone. His confederates under his trusted lieutenant Ali Yusuf were scouring the city – police, private and public CCTV databanks for a glimpse of her. But she was too clever, too subtle for even his sophisticated crew.

There were times when, were she not a girl, Achmed would admit his sister's brilliance.

But she was a girl. And her place was at home.

So had decreed their father, the sheikh. And the clock was ticking on Achmed's position as favored son. He had thus far to turn up his kidnapped sister. And there were other brothers, cousins waiting in the wings. Each had their own reasons for wanting to see him fail. This was a thing Achmed was determined to deny them.

He was crown prince. It was for him alone to secure the family's honor. It was his duty and obligation to prevent shame upon his house by bringing his sister Aisha home. And bring her home he would.

And so he had developed and followed a plan. Early in the day, he cruised the waterfront cafés and bistros frequented by breakfast customers. Then he drove around the shopping district, concentrating on clothing stores. When lunch came, he returned to the cafés and bistros, scanning. When he found nothing, he bought a falafel at an outdoor stand and contacted Ali Yusuf. He and his teams were having no better luck.

The prince was about to call it a day when he decided to make one more pass by the waterfront. Pulling up at a crosswalk near the beach, he glanced at the array of flesh visible on the sand. It was off-season, so there were fewer bikinis in view but Achmed's eye was not drawn to such sights. He didn't want to admit It to himself, but he found the sight of the beach and the ocean more pleasing. The West, with its many temptations, was a grotesque distraction.

That's when he saw her.

It wasn't even the features of the woman visible on the pier but that distinct flick of the shoulder as she turned. A brother knows his sister, even at a distance. She was turning from the SUV she had just stepped out of and turning toward the pier.

The light changed and he coasted ahead, careful to keep her in sight. The traffic thickened near the docks. He was able to coast slowly, concealed by the other cars as he surveyed the pier. Yes, *there!* Aisha and the woman he recognized from DC, the one who had cut Ali Yusuf. And close by ...

*Cody.* Achmed was sure of it!

He noted the shape and position of the ship they boarded and turned onto the pier at the next available light. He cruised along the row of parking reserved for ship owners and passengers, slowing as he passed the yacht. He read the name, *Lorelei*, inscribed on the hull and smiled. Then he pulled back into traffic and thumbed the speed dial on his cell to alert Ali Yusuf.

He had them now.

# CHAPTER THIRTY-FOUR

"FATHER VINCENT successfully tunneled his way into the casino CCTV system." Turnois took a seat beside Valachi in the first row of pews. All around them, the interior of St. Nazaire was cool and dark. "More footage of your Monsieur Cody. He, too, found his way to the second-floor security office."

"A thorough man!"

"He would have made a good Jesuit." Turnois spoke with grudging admiration. "He pretended to be a courier. Didn't get inside. Although we got a look at his vehicle. And a partial license."

"Go on ..."

"Our friend at the marina mentioned a man named Jacquard. Such a man operates a large bakery here in the city. He has a car whose plate matches the partial."

"Excellent," replied Valachi. "To find the princess, we must find Cody. To find Cody, we follow Jacquard. Put a tail on him."

"I'll see to it personally, father."

"Good."

---

TURNOIS TURNED the corner into the alley behind the grocery store. As suspected, the young produce employee whom he'd seen duck out back stood there smoking among a clutch of dumpsters. Turnois approached with a smile.

"Allo, bonjour," he said to the young man. "How are you? Pardon, but do you know this area of town? I'm lost."

"Sure thing, father." The young man spread his hands. "How can I help?"

"Some directions, please." Turnois' eyes flicked to the cigarette in the boy's hand. "And could you possibly spare a cigarette?"

"Certainly, father." The boy drew a pack from his pocket. His attention was on opening it when Turnois delivered a vicious chop to the neck. When the boy fell, he was ready to grasp shoulders and drag the body behind a dumpster.

Five minutes later, Turnois stepped onto the sales floor, his priest collar gone and shirt open, wearing a produce apron. The store was crowded with customers and employees so he had very little trouble blending in. But a manager with a clip board shot a puzzled glance at him.

"You are new? With Pierre in fresh produce?"

"*Oui, monsieur,*" said Turnois obediently.

The manager made a sound of exasperation. "Take that box there and drop it off at the customer service desk on your way past, please."

"*Certainement.* Yes, sir." Grateful for the prop, Turnois grabbed up the box, shouldered it and went looking for Jacquard.

He had followed the Frenchman here from the yacht. Turnois wanted to catch a glimpse of his car, get a sense of how large the party might be for which he provided shelter. What better way than to watch him shop for groceries?

*An army marches on its stomach,* Turnois thought, recalling his days in the Foreign Legion.

He moved to the front of the store, walking past the cash registers and looking up each aisle as he passed. The thickness of the crowd made it difficult. He had almost reached the end of the aisles and was preparing to make another pass when he spotted the man.

Jacquard was in the meat section, bent over a freezer of steaks and ground beef. This area was right next to the produce section, so Turnois set down his box and began loading its contents onto a nearby shelf, watching Jacquard as he did. The Frenchman's cart was piled high, and he worked from a handwritten list that he held in his hand. Turnois studied the contents of the cart.

Jacquard might as well have been shopping for a large family. There was enough food in the cart to feed several adults and children. *So onboard the yacht is more than just Jacquard,* he thought. Turnois guessed Cody, possibly Aisha and at least one other adult were staying there on a semi-permanent basis. *And Jacquard?* Hard to say with that much food…

"You idiot. I told you to get that box to customer service!"

The manager with the clipboard had spotted Turnois and was approaching. In the split second between his hearing the raised voice and Turnois mustering a response, Jacquard started and looked over. In time to catch Turnois watching him.

"Idiot! Lottery tickets don't go in the produce section!"

"So sorry, monsieur." Turnois ducked his head subserviently and began putting tickets back in the box. *Damn, damn, damn!* he thought as Jacquard grabbed his cart and made a beeline out of the meat department.

Turnois hustled the box over to the customer service desk, dropped it off and went to resume surveillance on his quarry.

Jacquard's wind was up. When Turnois found him again, the Frenchman was in the baked goods section, sweeping his quarters every few seconds: twelve, six, three, nine ... twelve, six, three, nine... Turnois had bungled the job and allowed himself to be burned. He wouldn't repeat the mistake.

Time for a change of wardrobe.

He flicked off the apron, tossed it onto a shelf and looked around. An elderly man had removed his cardigan and hung it over the handlebar of his shopping cart while he went off to examine merchandise. Turnois lifted it casually, put it on and struck off after Jacquard.

The man had made his way toward the cash registers, joining a long line. As usual, not all registers were in use, creating a clogged congestion of people around the tills. Turnois grabbed a can of beans from a shelf and stood in the line beside Jacquard's, several spaces back from the Frenchman with his hoard of groceries.

*We know what he's bought. Next, we'll get a fix on the vehicle he's currently using and tail him to his residence,* thought Turnois. From that point forward, it would be an easy matter of conducting an insert operation and eliminating Cody and his team.

"On break already?" The clip board man was back, hassling Turnois. "Did you deliver the lotto tickets?"

"Yes, sir," stammered Turnois. "I just –"

It was as far as he got. Jacquard, recognizing the manager's tone, turned, saw Turnois and abandoned his shopping cart, vanishing into the crowd streaming toward the exits. Turnois made an excuse and went after him. But by the time he had reached the street, Jacquard was gone.

# CHAPTER THIRTY-FIVE

Le Nid de Rats was, if not the lousiest dive bar in Monte Carlo, surely a runner-up. Crammed into a low-ceilinged building between a mortuary and a furniture fabric store, the "Rat's Nest" (as it was called in English) played host to the roughest crowd in a town not known for much street crime or scruffy inhabitants at all. Sitting across the street from it in Jacquard's car, Cody thought the place would look right at home in Phoenix or Fort Worth – anyplace where the rough and tumble of American city life met the wrong side of the tracks. They were here to verify a possible underworld connection between Thelma Justice and her team of Russians at her airport hangar.

"There is no doubt about it," Jacquard complained. "It is now official. Someone has set up surveillance on me."

"You're sure?"

"No doubt." Jacquard made an abrupt cutting motion with his hand. "I have been in this business a long time, monsieur. Since before you were born. Since de Gaulle was president! I met him once, you know."

"My condolences."

"Guard your tongue, monsieur. President de Gaulle was one of the greatest heroes France ever produced!"

"As he never failed to remind anyone he came into contact with. What's this about your being shadowed?"

"It's beyond a doubt." Jacquard crossed his arms and glared out the window. "I began feeling that tingle in the back of the neck. You know the one – the feeling that lets you know you are being watched. And then, earlier, in the supermarket. A man masquerading as an employee followed me."

"That is significant." Cody mentally sorted through a list of possible enemies. "Was he Middle Eastern?"

"No. French."

"French? You heard him speak?"

"Not very clearly," Jacquard admitted. "But he had the bearing of a Legionnaire. I can spot those types a mile away."

Cody filed the piece of data away in his mind. "Could be Achmed's bought spy. Or the Vatican. Or Vetrov and Thelma Justice. Either way, we won't get answers sitting here." He tugged the inside door handle. "Let's go see what we can find out inside."

They crossed the street and entered the Rat's Nest. The place more than lived up to its name. The atmosphere was dark and redolent with the distinctive dive bar odor of bleach. Mismatched memorabilia festooned the walls – posters from rock shows, old boxing photographs and (for some inexplicable reason) a fishing net with crossed harpoons. Cody wondered if the place might once have done duty as an oyster bar. A half-dozen desperate types crowded the bar, a scruffy collection of bikers, construction workers and other lowlifes. Cody drew Jacquard to the far end.

The barman came over, heard Cody's mangled French and immediately switched the conversation over to English. "What can I get you?" he asked. He flicked his gaze dubiously to Jacquard. In his cloth cap, hunting jacket and tailored shirt, the Frenchman was about as far away from typical clientele as the Rat's Nest got.

"Two beers, please." Cody leaned across the bar on his elbows. "And some information."

"What kind of information?" The barman's look was hard and suspicious as he began pulling a draft from a nearby tap.

"My friend here…" He hooked a thumb at Jacquard. "He's looking for work."

"I'm not an employment agency," said the barman. He set down the first draft, its head wobbling, and picked up an empty glass. "Have you checked the wanted ads?"

"Alas, we have." Cody spread his hands. "But my friend here is in a rather specialized line of work."

"He's also kind of fat. Old and fat. They don't tend to hire old and fat these days."

"Like I said. My friend is in a specialized line of work."

"Which is?"

"He's a baggage handler." Cody shot a glance at Jacquard's gold watch and revised that. "Actually, he supervises baggage handlers. Did so for years in, ah, Belgium. We're interested in any contacts you may have at the airport."

At this, the group of men chattering fell silent. Six pairs of eyes narrowed and slid Cody's direction. One of the men, a biker from the look of him and the meanest, dirtiest lout of the bunch, stood and strode over to them.

"You come in here asking questions about the airport?" The biker, growling his words through a Francophone English accent, halted before Cody and crossed his arms. "Baggage handling at the airport is ours, it belongs to the Bandits and our members. No outsiders welcome. Who do you think you are?"

"Are any of your members Russian?" Cody asked innocently.

At this the biker's eyes shot wide and he spat on the bar room floor. "Damn Russians! They only work in one hangar! And to hell with them! Now you better leave before I put your head through a wall."

Cody saw the twitch – that classic pre-motion electrical charge that surges through every guy before a fight – and moved first. While the biker was still raising his fist to deliver a blow, Cody waded in with a classic two-elbow strike: one to the midsection, crumpling him, and the other to the back of the head, bringing him to the ground.

Three of the remaining five at the bar rushed him. Cody blocked the first one's punch and winded him with a blow to the solar plexus. The second tried a kick, which he intercepted and turned against the man. The third he kicked savagely between the legs, reducing him to a howling, puking wreckage writhing on the ground.

Cody turned to the remaining two sitting at the bar. Opened his eyes wide and rolled out his palms as if to say, *Well? Are you guys coming or not?*

The two men exchanged glances, rose with their drinks and moved to a far table.

Cody wasn't aware that the bartender intended to make a play until the man was almost on top of him. A great crash and splintering of wood sounded behind him and Cody turned to see the barman face down on the ground, bleeding from his skull.

Over him stood Jacquard, holding the splintered remains of a barstool.

Cody chuckled, to which Jacquard took offense.

"I would not be a very good host, monsieur, if I allowed my guests to get pummeled on an outing!" He dropped the remains of the stool on the ground. "I suggest we concentrate our efforts elsewhere."

"Good idea," said Cody.

# CHAPTER THIRTY-SIX

"WE HAVE A LEAD ON JACQUARD." Turnois sounded
excited as he took a seat beside Valachi in the pew. "It
turns out that we have a source very close to him. *Very*
close."

"Who?"

"His brother-in-law works for us." Turnois smiled.
"He is a priest attached to the Archbishop's office. He
works in the diocesan archives."

"Bring him to me."

"I have him outside." Turnois rose and went to a
door. He opened it, spoke briefly to someone in the
other room and then returned, a middle-aged priest in
tow. "Father Valachi, this is Father Rodin. Father Rodin,
Father Valachi is the head of the Order of St. Adrian and
my superior. He would like to ask you several questions."

"Of course." The priest, obviously flustered by this
strange meeting, did a good job of concealing his
nervousness. "How may I be of service?"

"I would like to ask you some questions, Father
Rodin. Please understand that I ask under the authority of

Cardinal D'Agostino of the Holy See. This conversation is and must remain entirely confidential. You understand?"

"Yes, father."

"Good." Valachi smiled. "Please be at ease, Father. Answer fully and no harm will come to you."

Rodin swallowed hard and nodded.

"You are related to a man who lives in Monte Carlo. A man named Alain Jacquard."

"I am, father. My brother-in-law. But he's an atheist. I can't imagine why the Church would –"

"We have our reasons. Jacquard runs a bakery, I understand."

"Correct, father. On la Rue des Bains, in the old part of town."

"And where is Monsieur Jacquard likely to be at this hour of the night?"

"In his office, father. He routinely works late."

Valachi turned to Turnois. "Assemble the team."

———

ACROSS TOWN in his hotel room, Prince Achmed roused himself from a doze and grabbed at the telephone jangling on the bedside table. He had requested a long distance, person-to-person call be dialed on his behalf by the switchboard. This would be it coming now.

"Sir, I have your call to the Emirates on hold and waiting for you. Please hold the line."

Achmed drew several deep breaths, then sat up and swung his legs over the edge of the bed. As always, he needed to psych himself up before having a conversation with Selim, his brother, second in line to the throne and thorn in his side since boyhood. He fought a groan as he waited for the exchange to click into place and his brother's voice to come on the line.

"*Salaam aleikum,*" said Selim, voice thin with static and distance.

"*Aleikum al-salaam,*" said Achmed. "My brother, how are you?"

"Ah, brother. What can I say?" Selim's voice fell into the familiar condescending, sing-song cadence he used whenever ribbing his older brother and oldest rival. "The duties and obligations a son owes to his father are monumental. How well we discharge these speaks to our spiritual stature. But of course, not all sons love their fathers…"

"It is a son's obligation to do his father's bidding." Achmed smiled nastily. "If he is capable, that is. And so I, as the oldest and strongest of the family's sons, have gone to bring our sister back home. This business occupies the majority of my attention, brother. I am very pressed. You called and left a message that you needed to speak to me. May I ask regarding what?"

Selim hesitated and Achmed braced himself for another volley of derision and mockery. But when his brother spoke again, his voice was soft.

"Achmed. Our father is dying."

"He has been dying for a long time, brother…"

"No, Achmed. He *is*. He's taken a turn for the worse. He's slipping fast and the doctors say he hasn't more than a few days before…"

Achmed bit his lips.

"He is asking to speak to you, Achmed. You must return home."

"No." Achmed shook his head. "He would not want that. He would prefer me to remain here and complete my mission. He was very clear on the importance of bringing Aisha home. I will remain and –"

"Brother…"

"And *you*, brother will arrange a video conference call between us for tomorrow. At father's convenience. Call me anytime day or night at this number and I will speak to father confidentially over the internet."

"Achmed…"

"It is a younger brother's job to honor the wishes of his elders. You will do this for me, Selim."

A knock came on the hotel room door.

"I…will do as you ask, Achmed."

"Very good. *Salaam.*"

Achmed hung up and went to the door. Drawing it wide, he saw the figure of Ali Yusuf, his most trusted right hand.

"*Salaam,* my prince." He bowed. "I trust I am not disturbing you…"

"*Salaam,* Ali Yusuf. Please come in."

Ali Yusuf entered Achmed's room. He was a thick-set, burly man with classic Arab features. Before his term of service with Achmed, he had worked as a mercenary contractor for a dozen Gulf heads-of-state. Bearded, hawk-eyed, he radiated menace, his burly muscles crowding the fabric of his tweed blazer.

"My prince, I come bearing news. I managed to get information regarding the boat. It seems it is the property of the American CIA. A craft specially designed for intelligence missions."

Achmed raised his eyebrows. "It makes one wonder what Cody has planned."

"Indeed. And what is more…" Ali Yusuf produced a photograph. "This man is most closely connected with the ship. He appears to be its caretaker. One of our brothers recognized him. His name is Alain Jacquard. He was with the French SDECE and then later Deuxieme Bureau. He is an intelligence veteran of many decades' service, now retired."

"Excellent work, Ali Yusuf. You serve your prince well."

"I thank you. And there is more." Ali Yusuf smiled. "We know where he is right now."

Achmed grinned. "Assemble the team."

# CHAPTER THIRTY-SEVEN

RUE DES BAINS was quiet in the late evening. The massive bakery had released its final shift of workers for the evening and the surrounding shops and restaurants were closed. In true baker's fashion, the morning shift would arrive at 3 AM to begin preparation of the day's product. But for now, all was quiet.

A line of black Peugeots rounded the corner and began creeping toward the back door of the bakery. As the lead car came within 100 yards of the door, it doused its lights. The rest of the column followed suit. The vehicles remained there, silent, somnolent – like a column of sleeping beetles.

From the opposite end of the street, another column of vehicles arrived. These were military-style Humvees, three in all. Like the Peugeots, they crawled along the dark street in a column, headlights on until the lead car switched its off. They parked 100 yards from the door on the opposite side of the street, leaving 200 yards between the lead vehicles in each column.

The driver and passenger side doors of the lead Peugeot opened. Valachi and Turnois emerged. They met at the front of the car.

"I don't like the look of that." Turnois flicked his chin at the line of Humvees.

"I don't either," muttered Valachi. Something didn't feel right.

———

BEHIND THE WHEEL of the lead Humvee, Ali Yusuf held his breath and examined the two figures in black conferring in front of the Peugeot.

"I do not like the look of this, my prince," he said.

"Nor do I," replied Achmed. During the drive here, his mind kept drifting back to his father. But now that they were in position to move, he was sharp and laser-focused. "Body guards, perhaps?"

"I do not think so, my prince." Ali Yusuf nodded toward the line of cars. "Why would men entrusted to protect someone conceal their presence and approach so stealthily? No. These men are likely police. Or criminals of some kind."

"Alert the team to remain where they are," said Achmed. "Let us go out and take a look."

"As you wish, my prince."

The two men opened the doors and stepped out of the lead Humvee. Achmed kept his eyes fixed on the two dark figures before the Peugeot. "We will walk calmly toward the back door of the bakery," he muttered to Ali Yusuf. "And we will see how these men react."

"Yes, my prince."

———

"THEY'RE COMING THIS WAY…"

"Let's remain calm, Turnois. Relax and light up a cigarette. We're just two friends having a chat on a quiet street at night."

Tournier produced his cigarettes, lit two and handed one to Valachi. They stood smoking, affecting a conversation about soccer as the two figures approached.

———

JACQUARD WAS WORKING in his upper-floor office when the sound of gunfire erupted in the street below. The moment the first shot fired, his hand snaked across the desk to extinguish the banker's lamp there, plunging the office into darkness. In a rehearsed series of movements, he remained sitting in his wheeled office chair as he rolled it backwards, pushing with his heels until he was concealed between two large steel filing cabinets. A smart move: no sooner had he concealed himself there than a bullet shattered the glass window and whined through the office.

Jacquard sat patiently, waiting, as the crashing din rose and crested outside. He heard a mix of small arms and semi-automatic rifle fire and screams in several languages. Whoever it was out there, they were "going big," as the Americans put it. Volley after volley of weapons fire rolled up from the street, intermixed with the sounds of yelling voices and shattering glass.

Then the rhythm of the weapons fire slackened, becoming more sporadic. Just the occasional burst, and the odd shouted command. Feeling the coast was now clear, Jacquard rose from his chair and came out from between the two filing cabinets. Stepping across to his desk, he pulled open a drawer and removed a Beretta.

Cocking the weapon, he moved to the side of the window, pushed aside the curtain and peeked out at the street.

Two columns of vehicles were parked there, one on this side and one across the Rue des Bains. Dark shapes lay in the road. As Jacquard watched the lead car nearest him, a Peugeot, flicked on its lights, revealing the shapes in the road to be the bodies of men dressed in black. The sudden light was greeted by gunfire from across the street. Under an answering volley, two men dashed out and grabbed a third lying in the road. They dragged him back toward the line of Peugeots.

*Casualties are mounting,* Jacquard thought.

The team from across the street then affected a rescue. One of their team also lay in the no-man's-land between the columns of vehicles. Jacquard could see him writhing there, howling and bleeding out in the light from the cars. Gunfire: the nearest men ducked behind their Peugeots and hunkered down as the bleeding man was grabbed and hauled off the street.

The wail of police sirens rose in the distance.

The gunfight now over, the men nearest Jacquard were piling into their vehicles. Shouted commands rose among the smack of closing doors. Engines gunned and the line of black cars plunged forward into the shadows at the end of the street and disappeared.

The vehicles across the street – Humvees, so far as Jacquard could tell – also switched on lights and gunned their engines. The last wounded man was dragged through a door into the middle vehicle and the column took off, hurtling down the street in the opposite direction from the Peugeots. Jacquard watched until they disappeared.

*A gang turf war,* was his first thought. But his suspicious nature in no way accepted this as conclusive.

# CHAPTER THIRTY-EIGHT

"How many did we lose?"

"Three, my prince."

"And wounded?"

"Only Ali. And he is expected to recover."

"Good."

"They are ready for you, my prince."

"Thank you, Ali Yusuf."

Achmed settled himself in the padded chair at the head of the boardroom table. This branch of the Central Bank of Monaco came equipped with executive seating, elite service options and its own secure videoconferencing link. All Ali Yusuf had had to do was drop the word "Prince" in connection to his employer to set things in motion for Achmed's call with his father, the Sheikh.

Halfway down the long, kidney-shaped table, someone had positioned a large flatscreen monitor. The call was being managed by an operator in the next room. Achmed heard a series of digital chirps before the screen came to life with a sharp view of his father, Sheikh

Ahmed, lying in his hospital bed. They had a private medical facility in the family palace, and the greatest doctors in the world available for his use on call. But all that power and privilege could not keep life from fleeing his body.

"*Salaam aleikum,* my son. It is good to see you. But tell me why, as a father, I should not be angered by your refusal to honor my wishes and return home to speak to me face-to-face, as your brother Selim told you?"

"*Aleikum al-salaam,* dear father." Achmed pressed his hand to his chest. "I am heartbroken to hear of your condition and even more broken-hearted to disobey your wishes. But I am caught between honoring two requests from you, my sheikh. The second is to return home. The first is to retrieve Aisha."

At the mention of his daughter's name, the aged sheikh perked up noticeably. "Aisha? Is there any news? Are you any closer to finding her?"

"I have a good lead, father ..."

"Good!"

"And little doubt she will be found shortly."

"That is good." The sheikh grimaced as he adjusted his position in bed. "It is about your sister that I wish to speak. That you place such urgency on your assigned mission is a great comfort to a dying man. It is my hope to be reunited with her before I die."

"It is my hope too, father. I shall do everything in my power to make it so."

"That is also good." The aged sheikh's attention turned inward. He had obviously given much thought to what he was about to say. "My son, Selim shared with me some troublesome news. He tells me that your sister the princess was taken by an American, a man named Cody."

"Yes, father. The infidel Jack Cody was the one who attacked our warehouse, killing our men and kidnapping Aisha."

"My son, this man Cody must die."

Achmed held his breath, listening carefully.

"For any man to lay hands on the princess is inexcusable. For an infidel to do so is totally unacceptable and a grave insult to our royal house. You understand, of course…"

"I do, father. The code of honor established by our ancestors and followed by you and every sheikh before you informs my steps. This insult shall not go unpunished. I pledge upon my word to avenge this slight in your name and so restore honor to our house."

Upon hearing these words, the old sheikh relaxed noticeably. He nodded, closing his eyes as he did so, and kept nodding. A great weight had come off of his soul.

"My son, I am pleased. My faith in you has not been misplaced. The man who shall rule when I am gone is more than fit for the responsibility."

At these words, Achmed's heart beat faster. *"The man who shall rule when I am gone …"* His rise from crown prince to sheikh seemed suddenly guaranteed. But with excitement was mingled real sadness, for Achmed loved and revered his father.

*Such is life,* he thought. *The bitter comingled with the sweet.*

"I will find Aisha," he promised. "And I will kill this man Cody. All will be as you wish, father. It shall be done soon. I will personally bring my sister to your bedside."

"All is as I would wish. Hurry, my son."

"I shall, father!"

*"Salaam."*

The sheikh looked to someone off camera and nodded. His image winked out. A moment later, Ali Yusuf entered the room.

"It is well with my prince?" he asked.

Achmed drew a deep sigh. "It is well, Ali Yusuf. The sheikh has been very plain in his instructions to me. There is no question of his wishes. We will retrieve Aisha. And we will kill Cody, the American. It is the express wish of the sheikh."

"And so it shall be," replied Ali Yusuf, nodding.

"You are keeping the boat under observation?"

"I am, my prince. Since the security guard was relieved, there has been a great deal of coming and going on the part of the princess and her abductors. We wait only for an opportune moment to strike."

"Push the timetable up," replied Achmed. "Assemble the assault team and have them ready to move tonight. I will personally join the surveillance effort and follow Cody myself. When the right moment presents itself, I will strike and avenge this insult to our family's honor."

"As you say, my prince."

Achmed dismissed Ali Yusuf and made ready for departure. By his feet was a leather satchel which he drew up and placed on the table before him. Working quickly, he unzipped the case and folded it open. Inside lay two items.

The first was a flat black pistol that appeared no different from any other weapon of its type. But instead of bullets, the magazine held a quiver of feathered flechettes, each containing enough tranquillizer to immobilize a horse.

The second item was also a weapon, but much older and of a very different sort. The ornate handle and curved sheath concealed a wicked Middle Eastern *jambiya* – the curved blade common to Yemen and Saudi Arabia. Achmed's had been in his family for over a century, having been first blooded in the Arab wars of previous eras.

He would use the tranquillizer gun to immobilize Cody. And the *jambiya* to cut him into strips. The insult to his family's honor demanded no less.

# CHAPTER THIRTY-NINE

CODY ARRANGED a conference call with his Backchannel allies using the sophisticated video conferencing equipment aboard *Lorelei*. Parsons, ensconced in his secure priest-hole in Moscow, peeped out at them through his little round glasses. Jacquard lounged at the table with a cup of coffee. At Cody's request, Sara had taken Aisha below. He wanted to talk to her separately.

"So, we've confirmed a heavy Russian presence in town," Cody began. "These seem to be mostly underworld types. But we know there is a strong overlap between them and our pals in Russian intelligence. They're all over casino security, and blend in well with the Russian émigré community here in Monte Carlo."

"A good many of those will be legitimate workers," offered Parsons. "Lots of young Russians go abroad seeking employment, especially with the latest economic downturn in the Motherland. I'd guess many of those young people are approached for grooming, by both the *mefiya* and the SRV."

"There is foreign intelligence in town, too," Jacquard

confirmed. "But Horace is right. Much of their activity will be below radar because of how they work. Getting young Russian workers to eavesdrop on conversations or go through someone's luggage is easy with a little bribe money... Backed up by a threat or two against the family back home..."

"So, Thelma Justice is here. And when Vetrov arrives, he'll have plenty of cover to go to ground." Cody stretched back and clasped his hands behind his head. "We know the operation is called CERBERUS. Which also happens to be the make of the hazmat suits stored at Thelma Justice's compound."

Parsons gave a low whistle. Even the normally unflappable Jacquard seemed shaken.

"Question is ... what's he up to?"

"I may have something." Parsons sounded almost reluctant. "There's been an explosion of classified military radio traffic. All having to do with our favorite little town of Pochep. You remember. The chemical weapons storage site? It's been the subject of frenzied inquiry lately. At first, I thought perhaps someone had stolen chemical weapons. But then a bit of data shook itself loose. Quite troubling. Pochep was used as storage for assets from the Hummingbird program."

"Suitcase nukes." Cody stiffened. "What's the matter at Pochep?"

"Apparently there has been ... an incident." Parsons consulted his notes. "A military convoy arrived unexpectedly, commanded by one of Vetrov's allies, a Colonel named Pushkin. He entered the facility, held the staff at gunpoint and then emptied the place of Hummingbird units. He, like Vetrov, is now in the wind."

"So it starts to come together," said Cody. "Thelma and Vetrov are going in as partners on some big armaments deal. But the name of the op and those hazmat suits make me think they have something in mind other than turning a quick buck."

"This represents a major threat to the US and France, as well as our NATO friends," said Jacquard. "The presence of these units in such numbers can destabilize global security on a massive scale. Gentlemen, I think the time has come for us to inform our respective governments."

"Cody can't do that," said Parsons patiently. "As far as CIA is concerned, he and Sara have gone off the reservation. There are senior people at the Agency lying in wait for him and Sara to surface. Communications must be handled very carefully."

"Did the President say anything?" Cody asked.

"He did." Parsons paused. "He asked me to wish you good luck. "

———

HE FOUND Aisha sitting on a bunk in one of the converted staterooms. Although pretty and holding herself together well, he could tell she was haggard. She had been through a lot. Now she held the last piece of the puzzle he needed to try and understand. The connection between Thelma, the princess and the tablet would tell him a lot about what needed to happen next.

"How are you feeling?" he asked, taking a seat on the bunk across from her.

"I am alright, thank you, Mr. Cody." She pulled her eyes up from the ground and met his gaze with the confidence of a princess. "There is an awful lot going on. You and Ms. Durrell and Mr. Jacquard are very proficient in protecting us."

"It's my honour. Truly." Cody cleared his throat. "Princess, I think it's time we had a serious conversation about your motives here. I understand that your dad is a foreign head of state. And you should probably have legal representation made available to you, but I think you'll agree that we don't really have time for that. Even now, our enemies could be closing in on us."

"Our enemies. Our families..." She shook her head and shrugged. "I'll help in any way I can."

"Great. That's good." Cody sighed. "So you got your hands on the tablet. And you were a follower of Thelma Justice around the same time."

"I still consider myself her follower. In a way. Even after everything that's happened. She's..." Aisha struggled for words. "She's an important thinker."

"Why do you think so?"

Aisha gathered her thoughts for a moment before speaking. "In my country, even a woman of my station is held captive to her family's wishes. I had abundance, but no freedom. Thelma Justice speaks to women of all walks of life. She has found a language to unite us. At a powerful, biological level. Women instinctively understand other women who follow Thelma. Between us, there's a kind of perfect sisterhood of equality. And there's safety in numbers."

"Like Medieval knights."

"Yes, exactly. Exactly like Medieval – Wait, what are you saying?"

"Thelma Justice is the voice of women's power. The tablet speaks of women's power. So much so that the Knights Templar changed their method of worship and lifestyle, becoming a co-ed religious order complete with female knights."

"So you're suggesting Thelma Justice is trying to ultimately create a force like that? An army of women?"

"Wouldn't you say she already has?" Cody smiled. "Now the question is what she's planning to do with it. But this much is clear: you can't provide her with any more support. You have to pick a side, and ours is against hers. We'll give you time to make up your mind. But you need to stay here while I plan our next moves. Clear?"

She replied it was clear and remained sitting where she was as he let the room. She dropped again into the privacy of her own thoughts and was still sitting there a half-hour later when she heard gunfire erupt above-decks.

# CHAPTER FORTY

JACQUARD disembarked from *Lorelei* soon after Cody returned from belowdecks. He left the vehicle there for Cody's use and took an alternate route home, walking two blocks to board a bus that took him to an underground parking lot. Jacquard kept vehicles in a number of different spots around town for use by either himself or other agents as needed on a contingency basis.

He took the stairs down to the lower level. He was giving serious thought to breaking with the protocols of the informal network he and his friends called Backchannel and going directly to the DGSE to reveal what he knew. Thirty – *thirty!* - briefcase-sized thermonuclear weapons were loose somewhere in Europe. The havoc such weapons would wreak on the global order was unthinkable.

Once, during the early Nineties, Jacquard had been part of a multi-agency emergency response to a dirty bomb threat in Berlin. The crisis had never leaked, and the media never got wind of it, as was standard under such scenarios. But the fuse of circumstance had burned awfully close to the powder keg: he and his fellow agents had come within minutes of recommending the evacuation of the city. But thankfully, the crisis had been resolved.

Reaching the bottom of the stairs, he began walking through the dimly-lit garage. His Peugeot was parked in a far corner.

Of course, he understood the code under which he and men like Parsons had undertaken their work. They helped the agents of Allied powers, in advisory and support roles only. Operational decisions were left up to the agents in question. He would do as was expected of him. But he would wrestle his conscience over it.

*Movement?*

He came to a dead stop, squinting into shadow. Was somebody back there, moving quickly in the vicinity of his car? Or was it only his imagination?

He waited, breath held, counting to ten. And when he heard no more, he continued, relieved.

Jacquard would write down what he knew and put it someplace safe. Yes, he decided as he put his key in the driver's side door, he would at least do that much. Settling behind the wheel, he was still trying to decide whether or hand-write or type the report when he turned the ignition and the Peugeot erupted in a fireball of hellish light and sound that shook the entire building, echoing out to the street beyond.

———

ACROSS THE STREET, a cigarette lighter blinked in the shadow. A man leaned into the flame with a cigarette between his lips, a facial scar visible above the white of his priestly collar in the brief seconds before the lighter winked out.

# CHAPTER FORTY-ONE

AISHA HIT the ground as the *Lorelei's* lights went out and the gunfire ripped through the decks above. As a member of the Emerati royal family, she had received crisis and counter-terrorism training, been taught what to do in the event of a kidnapping or assassination attempt. But even now she found herself in a dilemma...

What if the attackers were from the Furies of Harmony?

If so, they would be looking for her. If the attackers were Achmed and his men, they would also be looking for her. And Cody had mentioned that a Vatican special operations team was also involved, and they would be seeking the tablet.

No matter who it was, they were looking for her.

Aisha dragged her messenger bag closer, looped the strap over her shoulder and reached inside. Jacquard had procured, with Cody's permission, a small automatic for her use. He had called the pistol a Ruby and said the handgun was old but reliable. Although only .32 calibre, it held nine rounds. Just holding it made her feel better.

Tucked next to the pistol, swaddled safely in a thick cloth, was the tablet.

How the relic had thrilled her when it came into her possession. How she had felt privileged, chosen by God. She had fallen on her face and prayed, praising God in the ancient words of her ancestors, comforted by them even as she was terrified of what the fragment's implications may be. For the powerful, the seated, those ensconced within the world's religious ecosystem, the fragment meant nothing but trouble. So, they meant nothing but trouble. For her.

Aisha gripped the pistol, came to her knees in the dark and crawled to the door.

Voices in the companionway outside. She recognized Ali Yusuf's:

"Go to the end of the companionway! Check every room!"

She had mere seconds in hand.

She cracked open the door. Ali Yusuf himself stood with his back to it. She held her breath, widened the doorway and raised the pistol until the muzzle was almost touching the back of Ali Yusuf's neck...

"Ali!"

At the cry from a man up the hall, Achmed's enforcer turned, raised the snout of the Uzi he carried and hurried off down the hall. Aisha used that opportunity to move into the darkened companionway and make for the stairs. She fled softly on bare feet, her shoes stuffed into her messenger bag, gun in her fist. She breathed a prayer of thanks Allah had spared her the task of killing Ali Yusuf. She crept up the stairs to the main deck.

An arm snaked around her throat, a hand covered her mouth and lips whispered in her ear:

"It's just me. Cody and Jacquard left twenty minutes ago. We're going to put you in the hiding place in the bridge stairwell. Got it?"

With that, Sara released Aisha. She turned and nodded. They began crossing the main lounge.

The assailant came out of nowhere. Clad in black, he brandished a naked blade and moved with the stealthy confidence of a predator. Sara pushed Aisha aside, flicked her right arm down hard and activated the spring-loaded sheath at her wrist. The titanium throwing knife leapt into her hand.

The assailant came down high toward her with a descending cut. Sara used her Systema training to evade and block, turning her maneuver into an attack with her own knife. Wielding the stainless throwing dagger like a switchblade, she ducked in, sliced her attacker's chest and slid back out again before he could respond.

But respond he did, after moving back to reposition and regroup. *He's not panicking,* Sara thought. Her assailant was a professional, perhaps even a foreigner. He moved like a ninja, and she thought she detected an Oriental slant to the eye that flashed close by her. They locked up briefly. The man broke free with one arm and tried to land a punch but she blocked. Then she threw a kick that connected with his stomach. The man in black folded, bowing forward. And her blade came down in the back of his neck, ending him.

The whole thing took place in complete silence and was over in seven seconds.

"C'mon." Sara breathed in Aisha's ear, pulling her up the steps. Voices came from the companionway below. Aisha looked back and saw the distant figures of Ali Yusuf and his men. Sara brought her halfway up the stairs and touched the decorative stud on the wall that activated the hidden doorway.

"Stay quiet," she whispered with a smile. Then the door closed and Aisha was alone.

# CHAPTER FORTY-TWO

"THEY'RE READY FOR YOU, Mr. President."

"Okay. Send them in."

President Harwood rose and stepped from behind his desk to greet the members of his national security crisis team. Harwood kept his crisis team small, with one representative each from the Joint Chiefs, CIA, Homeland Security and State. Also present was Dr. Simon, his National Security Advisor. He greeted her first, then the new JCS Chairman Admiral Ritter. Secretary Brown from Homeland Security and the Secretary of State were next. For some reason, Jared Parnell was once again sitting in for the Director. Harwood concealed his displeasure at this by gesturing for the team to occupy the couches and chairs before the Oval Office hearth.

"Thank you for coming," he said, settling in the rocking chair at the head of the coffee table. "Seems we've had an incident in Russia with serious ramifications. Doctor, if you would care to put us in the picture, please?"

"Yes, sir." Dr. Simon, a former Harvard professor whose plain looks belied a razor-sharp mind, removed her glasses and rubbed the bridge of her nose before addressing the group. "Defense Intelligence Agency confirmed signal traffic intercepted from Russian naval intelligence an hour ago. All Russian intelligence assets, civilian and military, have been activated and deployed in response to a break-in and theft at the military weapons storage facility in Pochep."

"Do we know what was taken?" asked Admiral Ritter.

"The Russians had a classified nuclear weapons development program called Hummingbird," she replied. "They had made serious strides in miniaturization tech, particularly in the area of centrifuges. The Hummingbird program enabled them to eliminate their bulky backpack tactical nukes for something more streamlined and easily concealed. The Hummingbird is a ten-kiloton nuclear weapon that can be carried in a small briefcase."

"Ten kilotons!" exclaimed Brown of Homeland Security. "That's ten times Hiroshima, isn't it? In a suitcase? And somebody's stolen one?"

"Correction," said Dr. Simon mildly. "They stole thirty of them."

Silence froze the room for several seconds.

"God," said Ritter quietly.

"Mr. President." Parnell smiled. "Sir, CIA has to take some of the heat for this. All our best intel points to General Vetrov and his colleagues. And we missed our best shot at him when we sent Jack Cody in to intercept that North Korean weapons deal and he failed."

"Failed?" Dr. Simon looked puzzled. "That's not how I remember things…"

"As I recall," said the President, "the shipment was intercepted and derailed. The sale never went through."

"But Vetrov escaped, sir." Parnell flexed his hands, his knuckles cracking as he did. He longed for a hit of his vape pipe but he was in the Oval. Plus, he was on a roll in his personal crusade against Cody. "Because of Jack Cody's negligence, Vetrov escaped and stole these suitcase nukes."

"Jack Cody?" Admiral Ritter squinted at Parnell quizzically. "Excuse me, Mr. Parnell, but Jack Cody is a highly trusted member of the special forces community. If Vetrov escaped, I'm sure —"

"It was entirely Cody's fault," interrupted Parnell. "Admiral, surely you agree. The Agency must be responsible for clearing up its own failures."

"Okay," said Harwood. "Let's get back on track here. I want a wildfire crisis team assembled and operating out of the National Military Command Center. All elements — intel, military and governmental — will report to the team leader. Secretary Brown, I need Homeland Security to tighten up any border loopholes and raise the terror threat level. We'll arrange for FBI counterterrorism to liaison with your team. The Secretary of State and I will get on the phone and start informing our allies in NATO and Five Eyes."

"Sir, it's worth noting -?"

"What is it, Mr. Parnell?" The President's annoyance with the man was palpable.

"Sir, we obviously have to protect the Homeland. But there's something we're missing here." Parnell turned and addressed the group. "Any type of nuclear blackmail scenario we've ever run has been a one-to-one threat response. Meaning: one group gets a bomb and threatens one government. But with thirty missing, that's all out the window, now."

"He's got a point, sir," said Dr. Simon. "If those bombs are deployed in multiple countries, whoever controls them will be in a position to put pressure on any government in the world. Imagine receiving a call instructing us to pull our carrier groups out of the Persian Gulf or risk London becoming nuked. Or Paris, if we don't remove missiles from Eastern Europe. Whoever is in possession of those bombs has enormous global leverage."

"Agreed," said Harwood crisply. "That's why my first call will be to the Secretary-General of NATO. We have to have a coordinated front on this. Work with our allies. And prepare for the worst. Okay. You have your marching orders..." Harwood rose, signalling an end to the meeting.

"Sir? One more thing." Parnell rose with him. "Sir, I'd like to request executive authority to put our special operations group on this."

"To do what, exactly?" Harwood asked. His patience with Parnell was at an all-time low.

"Find Vetrov." Parnell shrugged. "Eliminate the threat."

"I already have somebody on that," Harwood replied.

"Two heads are better than one, sir."

Harwood considered the offer. He had not heard from Jack Cody in several days. The crisis was massive and the United States was running out of options.

"I'll take it under advisement."

"Sir, I –"

"That will be all, Mr. Parnell. Thank you."

Harwood remained standing as the group left the

room. Then he went to his phone and got his Chief of Staff on the line.

"Put in a call to that Brit in Moscow," he instructed. "I need to find out where Jack Cody and Sara Durrell are right now."

# CHAPTER FORTY-THREE

THERE WERE CANDLES AND INCENSE. Flowers. And a love nest at the center of the room: pillows and blankets laid out on the floor, along with a tray of delicious wines and finger foods. Besides these were unguents and oils, lotions and toys of various shapes and sizes – everything necessary for a romantic rendezvous between the pair twined together in lustful embrace. Sweat and oils beaded their skins, making Thelma Justice's and Vetrov's bodies glow in the candlelight as they satiated their need at the center of a forest of silver briefcases, arranged around them in ever-widening circles.

Knowledge of the danger and power they represented fueled Thelma Justice's hunger. She spun mentally, heart thrashing in her chest as her Alpha lover brought her to the edge and she crested over in a delightful wave of pleasure.

Afterwards they lay together, talking.

"I can't believe we did it," she whispered. "Look at all these beautiful weapons. Weapons. And seeds, really. That's what they are."

"Seeds?" Vetrov chuckled. "Woman, you are crazy."

"Perhaps." She laughed, too. "But they *are* the seeds. Seeds must become destroyed in order for plants to grow. We're planting a garden, Greb. A garden for such beautiful flowers."

"Christian myths say the world began in a garden."

"Patriarchal myths," she spat. She sat up angrily, seized a goblet and downed a hard swallow of wine. "In our natural state, women lead. Who else? Women give birth. Women create fully actualized human beings from the raw material of children. Women are the creators of civilization. So it was and always will be. But the natural order has been short-circuited. By patriarchs, by men. Their work must be destroyed before mine – before *ours* – can commence."

"And so?" Vetrov leaned up on one elbow. "What is your plan?"

"These will be sold to various terror groups around the world. The majority will go to your jihadi friends in Syria. The bombs will be planted in cities around the world – most of them national capitals. Then we will begin to exert pressure. A threat here, a suggestion there... We may have to detonate one of these, but I doubt more than one. In either case, even if we have to detonate all thirty, we will. I have the equipment to send in my Furies as first responders to nuked cities, thus proving the value of my demands."

"Which are?"

"Control." She purred the word. "We will begin to impose a global government. Of women. The *real* Order of World Harmony. It will go from an idea to a reality. We will make it happen."

# CHAPTER FORTY-FOUR

AISHA STARTED AWAKE.

The hidden compartment where she sat was both water- and soundproof. The last thing she had heard as the door slid shut was a cry from Ali Yusuf. But if any gunfire had followed, it was cut off by the hatch closing. Sara had not returned. Aisha had no idea what had happened to her or how much time had elapsed since she had been placed here. She fumbled in her messenger bag, found her cellphone and checked the time.

*Nearly six AM!* Her heart hammered in her chest. She must have been more tired than she thought, having dropped off and slept for a few hours. Slipping her phone back into her messenger bag, she crept to the hatch and put her hand to the release knob. She pulled the spring-loaded knob, careful to keep hold of it lest the hatch pop wide. The catch released and she eased it open.

A dim sliver of gray light filled the crack. She felt her ears pop as the hold's pressure released. She smelled the residue of gunpowder and cordite, and the foul smell of death. But she didn't hear a thing.

She pushed the hatch open further.

The wall across the stairs had been ripped by gunfire. A scorched smell reached her nose and, as she moved further out, she could see the body of a figure in black lying on the lounge floor below. The assailant Sara had killed. Aisha recalled it with a shiver. She watched the figure long enough to ensure no movement, then snuck out onto the stairs and down.

The *Lorelei* was a shredded tangle of glass and wreckage. The gunfight had reduced the CIA's lovely yacht to a lamentable scow. Aisha felt a twinge of sadness about that loss. For, regardless of the purpose for which she had been built, the *Lorelei* was a thing of beauty. And, like all ships, she was a lady. There are few sadder sights than a lady in ruins.

Easing out of the compartment, she took the stairs down to the lounge, passed the body on the floor and then descended to the lower deck.

More bodies. All men. No sign of Sara.

She breathed a sigh of relief.

She crept to the window and peeped out. A ribbon dawn lit the sky to the east and the streets were silent. A police car sat nearby, its driver door open and its blue light twirling. Two cops stood talking quietly. They had obviously been dispatched to respond to the chaos. As Aisha watched, one officer patted another on the arm, pointed and then returned to the police cruiser. A moment later, he was pulling away from the dock.

*He's left the other behind to guard the scene,* she thought.

She studied the cop who had been left. He was obviously the junior partner of the two. Young, bleary-eyed, he had obviously been roused from a sound slumber to be hustled out to the docks this early. *They will be coming soon with detectives and a forensics team,* she thought. Until then, it was this boy scout's job to ensure nothing walked off before it could be catalogued.

The young cop coughed and huddled into his jacket, shivering. A distance away, a small food truck drove onto the pier. The cop watched as the owner opened up and got ready for the day's customers. Unable to resist the temptation of a hot coffee, the young cop dragged out his wallet and wandered over to the truck.

Aisha slipped back to the compartment, took up her messenger bag and shoes and returned to the lounge. Through the window she could see the pier. The cop and the food truck owner were examining something out on the water, their backs turned to *Lorelei.* Aisha slipped up on deck and over the side, landing softly on the pier with bare feet and running to take cover behind a pile of crates before the cop noticed. Putting on her shoes, she kept under cover, hugging the wall until she came to the stairs. She looked back over her shoulder.

The cop and the food truck guy had advanced to the water's edge and were staring out to sea, talking.

Aisha took the stairs to the street and crossed into the small neighborhood of shops and cafés there. One place with a patio was already open. She sat and ordered breakfast, careful to keep her back to the street. The streets came alive as she ate, the morning commuters and pleasure-seekers coming out in a trickle. By the time she paid her bill and left, it was full daylight. As she reached the street, she studied the docks. The area was now thick with police vehicles.

She thought of the item in her bag, of the danger it

posed to herself and her rescuers. She simply had to dispose of it. But how?

The solution came to her as she wandered the street. She paused outside a store advertising stationery and mail delivery services. Looking both ways before crossing the street, she went inside.

"*Bonjour*, good morning," she said to the clerk. "Can I mail a package from here?"

"Of course, mademoiselle," said the clerk. "We can do regular mail, courier package or registered delivery. What is your pleasure?"

"Registered delivery, please," she said. "I'll need a container and a sheet of paper and pen to write a note to include."

"Of course." The clerk put the requested items in front of her. "And where are we sending this package?"

"Switzerland," she said. "Zurich. I just need something delivered to some friends there."

"Of course." The clerk smiled, only too pleased to help.

# CHAPTER FORTY-FIVE

CODY SPENT the night staking out Thelma Justice's compound from the vantage point Jacquard had shown him. Utilizing some of the night-vision gear the Frenchman had stockpiled and provided for their use he conducted a careful, hour-by-hour study of movement within. Thelma Justice's organization was exceptionally well run. The Furies kept a tight watch on the place, backed up by another smaller group of black-clad soldiers cradling machine pistols. To Cody's surprise, these soldiers were male. But a scan of their weapons identified them as Russian.

*They move like Spetsnaz,* he thought. He knew the type well: professional Russian spec warriors who were every inch the Tier One operators that Navy SEALS, British SAS or Canadian JTF-2 were. These were no Russian gangsters pulling extra shifts. Their presence here confirmed Vetrov's.

Cody remained observing and taking notes for as long as he could. When dawn smeared the eastern sky, he rose and stretched. Packing up, he turned the car around and headed back down the hills toward Monte Carlo, arriving at the docks just as the police presence there was picking up.

The *Lorelei* was in shreds. Even from a distance, the damage from the attack was unmistakable. Shattered glass and broken fixtures littered the deck. *Sara? Aisha?* Mastering his panic, Cody parked by the stairs and strolled to the railing, playing the part of the curious rubbernecker. As he watched, two paramedics disembarked hauling a covered body on a stretcher. Cody remained calm as he pulled out his cellphone and texted Sara:

WHERE ARE YOU?

After pushing send, he cocked his ear to hear whether or not a ping would sound from the body under the sheet. It did not. And, to his relief, Sara replied a minute later:

AT THE HOSPITAL. AMBUSHED. AISHA'S BROTHER. AISHA TUCKED INTO HIDDEN COMPARTMENT. MANAGED TO LIQUIDATE THE HIT TEAM. JACQUARD HAS GONE DARK.

Not good.

After verifying that her wounds were minor, Cody replied he would join her at the ER shortly. He was about to turn away when something caught his eye.

Two men were disembarking from the boat in the company of a dog handler. Cody could tell right away these were no local detectives. Every detail from their tailored suits and sunglasses to the cool, clipped way they gave instructions to the cops identified them for what they were: DCRI, French domestic intelligence. If they had brought a dog onboard and were now disembarking without Aisha, it was a good bet she had weathered the storm and made her escape. He texted her next. She replied immediately:

ACHMED'S MEN ATTACKED THE LORELEI. I HAVE ESCAPED AND AM HIDING IN THE LOCAL LIBRARY.

Cody felt a swell of relief. After telling her to stay put, he turned and got back into the car.

He wasn't too worried about Jacquard. The crusty old Frenchman was a professional who could take care of himself. For now, his priorities were to secure Aisha and hook back up with Sara as quickly as possible. He used Google to locate the hospital and library. The former was closer and on the way to the latter so he drove there first.

He eventually found a nurse who spoke English and was conducted by security to the emergency room. He found Sara sitting, legs dangling over the edge of a gurney in a curtained-off section of the ward. She was still clothed and quite conscious, her wounds consisting of a cut hand and a pretty nasty shiner on her right eye. Otherwise, she was in top form. She quickly relayed to him the circumstances of last night's attack.

"I just came from the docks," he said. "The cops are crawling all over what's left of *Lorelei*. And I saw some domestic intelligence types there. So the French are hip to the ship's status as a CIA control vehicle. Fortunately, they didn't find Aisha."

"She's okay?" Sara winced as she stood.

"Yeah, she's fine. She made it to the local library and is hiding out there."

Sara shouldered her purse. "Let's go get her."

It was a short drive. Sara texted ahead, so Aisha appeared at the doorway the moment they pulled up in front. She got into the back seat and Cody pulled back into traffic.

"Are you alright?" Sara asked.

"I am, thank you." Aisha sighed. "I was worried they might have..."

"It's okay." Sara smiled. "I'm just glad you're not hurt."

Aisha stared out the window, obviously unsettled, silent for a while. Then: "Achmed is going to be furious. You killed half his men."

Cody smirked at Sara. "Only half? You're losing your touch."

Sara chuckled. "So where to now?"

"I'm thinking Jacquard will show up at his bakery. We'll go there first."

Cody navigated the narrow stone streets of the historic neighborhood where Jacquard had his business. Jacquard had mentioned starting the bakery as a lark, out of the boredom brought on by retirement. But success had found him anyway. Now he and his staff supplied fresh product to restaurants, hotels and casinos throughout town. A nice revenue stream that also provided handy cover for his activities with the Backchannel.

They turned onto the street where the bakery was located. Cody spotted a handful of white clad bakers out front, clustered together and talking seriously. As they parked, he saw one woman with red eyes snatch off her hat and bury her face in it. He wondered if perhaps some kind of workplace accident had occurred. Something was obviously very wrong.

"What's up?" asked Sara as they approached.

"Monsieur Jacquard is dead," replied one of the men. "We just saw on the TV news this morning!"

Cody's guts chilled. "How?" he asked.

"It was a freak accident, monsieur," replied the baker. "His car apparently caught fire. There was an explosion and..."

"Freak accident, my ass," muttered Sara.

The cellphone in Cody's pocket pinged. Someone from an unidentified number had texted him a video. He opened it.

Blackness onscreen faded into the image of a car engulfed in flames. The top of the blaze flattened against the roof of an indoor parking garage at night. The car burned fitfully for a few seconds before the image faded to be replaced by the words:

I WILL CALL YOU SHORTLY, MR. CODY.

And then his phone rang.

# CHAPTER FORTY-SIX

"CODY HERE."

After a longish silence, a gravelly voice spoke. "Did you enjoy the video, Mr. Cody?"

After a parting glance at the group by the bakery door and a nod to Sara, Cody moved a short distance away. "I don't enjoy snuff films," he replied.

"You see what happened to Monsieur Jacquard. He was at crossed purposes with our cause and paid the price. The question now is: will you?"

Cody's patience snapped. "Who is this?" he demanded.

"The rightful owners of the tablet in Princess Aisha's possession want it back," said the gravelly voice calmly. "You must understand, Mr. Cody, there are authorities in this world that transcend those of governments and individual liberty. Authorities which pre-date the existence of most modern countries. Authorities which serve beneath the banner of the crossed keys of Peter."

"The Church." Cody said it flatly. He had heard rumors of Vatican operatives, of a clandestine counterintelligence service so ancient and secret that its very existence was a rumor. Even the CIA itself, which cultivated alliances with allied intelligence services worldwide, encountered a locked door when they knocked at St. Peter's.

"I serve he who wears the Fisherman's shoes, yes." Cody thought he heard a note of satisfaction in the man's voice. "Our Order is very close to the throne of Peter. And our instructions are clear. We are to recover the tablet. I will contact you with instructions for delivery soon, Mr. Cody. And I warn you. The arm of the Church is long. And the hounds of the Inquisition, once loosed, cannot be called back. Do not resist us."

The man hung up. Cody stood shaking with rage for a long moment before regaining control of himself and returning to Sara's side.

"Who was that?" she muttered.

"The man who put the bomb under Jacquard's car," he said calmly. "It seems, in addition to Vetrov and Thelma Justice, we also have the Roman Catholic Church to contend with."

"A Vatican hit team?" She sounded as surprised as she did skeptical.

"You know they have the capability. So do I. The surprise is that they were resourceful enough to identify a retired French intelligence agent and the fact that he was assisting us. That takes some reach."

"What do they want?"

"What do you think they want?" he asked. He turned to Aisha. "Did you bring the tablet with you?"

"Yes. But it is no longer in my possession," Aisha said. "I've hidden it."

"Where?"

She smiled. "Someplace safe."

A sting of annoyance nettled Cody. He started to answer but then paused. It occurred to him that Aisha didn't owe them complete transparency. Not on this – or any – issue. Their alliance wasn't formal. And, in either case, the fewer people who knew the location of the tablet, the better.

"Is it someplace where you can retrieve it easily?" Sara asked.

"I can retrieve it," Aisha answered. "But not easily. It's no longer in France. That is all I will say."

"Okay." Cody smiled and put a hand on her shoulder. "That was a smart move on your part. Thank you."

He thought he might have actually seen her blush. Sara smiled and nodded, agreeing with him. Their progress might go just that much smoother with the tablet out of their possession and stored someplace safe. They didn't need the relic to stop Vetrov.

The sound of a motorcycle intruded as it turned the corner and started down the street toward the bakery. Cody looked up. A uniformed bike courier braked to a stop at the curb beside them. He flipped up the visor of his motorcycle helmet and produced a clipboard.

"Delivery," he announced to the group. "For a Mr. Cody?"

Puzzled, Cody stepped forward. "I'm Cody."

"Sign here, please."

Cody took the courier's pen and initialed the blank space on the delivery manifest. The courier handed over a sealed manila envelope, its flap double-secured with masking tape.

"The Backchannel has you, Mr. Cody," said the courier with a wink. Then he sped off up the street.

Cody and Sara exchanged a look.

"Well. What is it?" she asked.

He tore open the envelope. Inside was a set of house-keys, a flash drive and a handwritten note.

IF YOU ARE IN RECEIPT OF THIS, I HAVE BEEN KILLED. GOOD LUCK. - J.

P.S. INSTRUCT RENÉ NOT TO BURN THE CROISSANTS FOR A CHANGE, PLEASE.

"Intel from beyond the grave," Cody replied.

He had to hand it to Jacquard. The man was thorough.

# CHAPTER FORTY-SEVEN

THERE WAS a tag with an address on it attached to the housekeys. They called a cab from the bakery and gave the address to the driver who drove them down the cobbled backstreets of old Monte Carlo to a neighborhood of quaint cottages. The area reminded Cody a bit of the suburbs back in the US except that, with few exceptions, the buildings were all at least three decades old. The streets were unbelievably quiet. Not a single soul was on the sidewalks and not a single curtain stirred when the three of them got out and took the walkway to the front door of one small cottage.

Inside, a stone-floored living room with a great iron hearth greeted them. Beyond lay a windowless kitchen with a rough deal table and a gas stove. Cody sat, examining the flash drive curiously. "Aisha, do you have your laptop?"

"I do." She set down her messenger bag and extracted a laptop. Booting it up, she accepted the flash drive and slid it into a port. The file window showing the drive's contents flashed onscreen. Cody saw several docu-

ments, a few .jpeg files and a text flat file marked
READ ME.

He tapped it with a fingernail. "Let's start here."

Aisha double-clicked the icon and a message
appeared.

> *This data packet has been prepared for delivery by courier*
> *to Backchannel as a redundancy in the event of my death*
> *or capture. Enclosed on this drive is information*
> *regarding an evolving terror threat in the Mediterranean*
> *region with connections to Monte Carlo and the Russian*
> *presence in our city.*

"As thorough as ever," said Cody. "Aisha, go ahead
and arrange those documents by date and open the
earliest one first, would you?"

The girl bent to her computer, fingers flying over the
keyboard. Once the documents were aligned by date, it
was obvious that Jacquard had been working on this
investigation for about a month prior to their arrival.
Aisha opened the first document. It was a three-page
report in French, the pages crammed with info in a small
font. Sara, whose French was better than Cody's, sat
forward and scanned the document briefly before letting
out a low whistle.

"Crimson Jihad," she whispered. "My God ..."

"I don't know them," Cody admitted.

"They're new." Sara finished scanning the document
and sat back. "An emerging jihadi micro-movement. A
splinter group from ISIS-K. They were apparently too
violent for -"

Aisha abruptly stood. Cody saw raw hatred smouldering in her eyes. Before Sara could finish, the girl

muttered something angrily in Arabic and stormed into the bathroom, shutting the door behind her.

"What's wrong with Aisha?"

"Crimson Jihad is responsible for the assassination of her uncle Fahd." Sara stared down at her lap. "He was a tireless ambassador for peace in the Middle East. God knows how many wars he prevented with his shuttle diplomacy. Any hour of the day or night, he'd jump aboard his private Lear jet and fly to Riyadh, Tel-Aviv, Tehran. Anywhere to stop a war. Crimson Jihad butchered him in a particularly awful way."

Cody knew about Prince Fahd. The man's reputation was second only to Kissinger's in terms of Middle East diplomacy. "I'd heard he was killed but I don't know the details."

"It was kept out of the news media," she said. "But they slow-tortured and killed him, butchering him *halal* style. They killed him the way Muslims butcher their meat. To send a signal that Crimson Jihad consider peace-makers to be animals."

Cody thought about that for a minute. It explained Aisha's rage. "Do they have much of a presence in Europe?" he asked.

"They're starting to. That's when they came on Langley's radar. A joint operation with British intelligence put us on the trail of a CJ operative in Germany. We almost captured him, too, with the help of German police. Had him cornered in a bed and breakfast. He blew himself up in the dining room along with ten other guests. Cody, we had information he was in contact with Group Red."

"Oh my God..." Cody knew them. "So they're..."

"Their split from ISIS-K was over CJ's obsession with weapons of mass destruction. ISIS has their share of scientists and labs working on things like Sarin gas and dirty bombs."

"But if CJ was in negotiations with Group Red then that means they've upped their game from dirty bombs." Cody knew Sara got it. Group Red captured top spot on the world's list of nuclear terror threats when they successfully hijacked a British military convoy carrying weapons-grade plutonium. They'd been selling off fragments of same piece by piece, much to the annoyance of INTERPOL and the western intelligence community.

"Given their obsession with nuclear weapons, if CJ has a presence here in town, then it's obvious who their Russian connection would be."

"Vetrov." Cody shook his head. "But why the hell would someone like Thelma Justice ever get involved with Islamic terrorists? They're sort of the opposite of feminist empowerment."

"The enemy of my enemy is my friend," Sara replied.

"In Monte Carlo, there seem to be plenty of enemies to choose from these days," he said. He felt a wave of sorrow imagining Jacquard furiously typing the report they now read in his upstairs bakery office. "And we've just lost one of the good guys."

# CHAPTER FORTY-EIGHT

ACHMED DROVE ALONG THE NARROW, winding mountain road in the pre-dawn dark. The road was only partially completed and hazardous, particularly at this elevation. Despite this, Achmed fought the urge to stab the accelerator and gain his destination in a roar of dust and engine noise.

The loss of his team aboard the yacht – Ali Yusuf in particular – gnawed at him like a living thing. Nevertheless, he was careful. *I've come too far, lost too much to throw it away now in a burst of impatience,* he thought. He reminded himself that he was a prince and that royalty never hurries.

And that, with royalty, ruthlessness was the coin of the realm.

He slowed to a bare crawl. The road crested up ahead. If he was right, this was the place to pause.

Achmed left the car running as he stepped out. The shoulders of the construction project were as yet a tangle of loose rock and dirt and his boots made just the barest crunch on the road gravel. Achmed took that path toward the crest, moving slowly, pausing now and then to crane up on his tiptoes for an advance view of what lay beyond the elevated section of road. He did it once, twice and then walked a little further on. About a hundred yards from the rise, he tried again.

There. The man he sought was just beyond the rise, with his back to Achmed.

The prince smiled. He had the quarry in his sights at last.

———

CODY ADJUSTED his position on the tarp he was using as ground cover and refocused his night-vision binoculars on Thelma Justice's compound far below. It would soon be light, but he wanted to get in a few more minutes of surveillance before the sun came up.

He had been reluctant to return for a third night of surveillance, knowing he risked exposure. Coming here had been a long shot, but it was a stone he could scarcely afford to leave unturned. He thought it unlikely he would spot any of the individuals identified in Jacquard's photos as Crimson Jihad operatives, but he had to make sure. No doubt they would soon make contact with Vetrov. And, for Cody's money, Vetrov's likeliest location at the moment was with Justice and her organization.

But the night was ending with no sign of Vetrov or any CJ operatives. He checked his watch. Dawn was twenty minutes away. Time to go.

Cody rose to his knees and tucked the bulky night-vision optics into its padded carrying case. Then he produced his cellphone and began composing a text to Sara.

STAKE-OUT IS A BUST. RETURNI -

It was as far as he got before a hammer-blow came down on his shoulder.

Achmed had managed to sneak up to within a few feet behind Cody. He had aimed the hard rubber cosh at the base of Cody's skull, intending to render him unconscious for later interrogation elsewhere. But Cody had tilted his head unexpectedly while composing the text so the blow had hit him hard on the shoulder, rattling the Vagus nerve at the top of the arm and jangling his mental switchboard.

Cody hit the ground, twitching, his vision blurring. *Who -?* For a moment, he thought he'd been spotted by the Furies. But then a rough-nailed hand grabbed him by the hair, pulled and suddenly he was staring into the snaring face of Aisha's brother, Achmed.

"You! Where is she? Where is my sister?" The prince's eyes were wide with rage, spittle foaming his lips. He dragged out a snub-nosed revolver and pressed it up under Cody's chin. "Tell me! Tell!"

Cody, his brain-stem still zapped by the blow, struggled to form words. Which was difficult, as his thoughts were a blur. He struggled to move his lips, to say something. But all he managed was a breathy grunt.

Achmed smacked him across the jaw with the butt of his gun. Cody crashed sideways to the ground, blood coating his lips and chin. Had he lost any teeth? He tried probing his mouth but his tongue wouldn't work.

"My sister," Ahmed snarled, "is a princess from a respectable, ancient line of Emerati kings! You have no business involving her in your filth! You will die for what you've done! Once I learn what I came here to know!"

Suddenly, Cody regained control of his mouth. A hiss of breath escaped his bloodied lips. Then: "J ... ja ..."

"What? WHAT?" Achmed again grasped Cody by the hair and shook.

*"Jam it up your ass, Achmed!"*

The prince blew his top. He shrieked, dropped his gun and punched Cody on the side of the head as hard as he could. Cody hit the ground, his skull throbbing, but still conscious. Achmed was stomping around in full meltdown, screaming and shaking his fists.

*This has got to be it,* Cody thought. How many times in life had he come this close to death? After nearly buying the farm on a dozen previous missions, it seemed his luck had just run out. He would die here on this deserted alpine road, his body cast into a ditch.

Achmed spun, marched over and snatched up his pistol. He kicked Cody in the ribs where he lay, forcing him to roll onto his back, face to the sky. Achmed loomed over him.

"Worthless infidel pig!" he screamed. "You dishonor my father! You dishonor my family! NOW! YOU! DIE!"

He extended the revolver at arm's length, snout pointing directly at Cody's forehead, and thumbed back the hammer. Then he paused.

A noise like a mosquito's whine broadened into the sound of a truck's engine. A few seconds later, Achmed heard truck doors slamming and the voices of a road crew arriving for work.

Abruptly, he regained control of himself. The crew would hear the gunshot, see him and then find Cody's body. They would see Achmed get into his car and drive away. They would note the license plate. Before too long, the police would track him down and an international incident of embarrassing proportions would erupt.

As much as he wanted to kill Cody now, he couldn't. Not even with a knife or his bare hands because he could hear the voices of the road crew approaching the rise below them.

He made a snap decision. Holstering his revolver, he pulled the small flat flechette gun from his pocket. It resembled an airsoft pistol. Cocking it, he aimed at Cody's neck and fired.

The tranquillizer dart felt like a dull thud to Cody when it hit. Moments later, his vision swam as the powerful drug took hold. His last vision of Achmed was a skewed, jumbled view like a shaky camera shot as the prince bent and grasped him by the shoulders. What...?

Achmed dragged Cody behind the vehicle he'd driven from Jacquard's house and left him there. Moments later, the road crew appeared. Achmed straightened and walked by them with a friendly wave. They didn't discover Cody until he reached his car. By the time they raised their voices in alarm, he had spun the ignition and started back down the mountain.

# CHAPTER FORTY-NINE

CODY LANGUISHED IN DARKNESS.

He was unafraid of the dark, or injury itself for that matter. He had long ago accepted a violent death as a relative certainty in his line of work. He didn't spend much time dwelling on it. Cody was not a man for religion or dogmas. He was a realist, and fatalistic into the bargain. Death was a bridge he figured he would cross when he came to it – a bridge that would reunite him with Carol and his kids. It was not an unpleasant notion. The problem right now, though, was being unsure whether or not he was dead.

He felt conscious. But was he? His brain commanded his body to move but it didn't. He felt his eyeballs shifting in their sockets, but the view above him never changed. It was like lying in a dark, shallow pond at night. He shifted his eyeballs again. A gnawing pain began in the back of his skull and his rediscovered his eye*lids*. With a tremendous effort, he managed to crack them open.

A fleshy blur hung above him. Two blinks and it

cleared, resolving into the shape of Sara's face. She was smiling.

"You are one lucky man, mister!" Relief flooded her voice. "The French roadcrew that found you said a man matching Achmed's description apparently drugged and threw you into a ditch. They found you just as he was leaving. One guy even jumped in his truck and tried to chase him down but Achmed lost him."

Cody blinked hard twice. Swallowed. "Tranqed me," he croaked.

Sara took up a cup of water from the night table and held the straw to his lips. "The dart left a lesion. The doc says it was some high-grade veterinary pharmaceutical. The thing they use to put racehorses under before doing surgery. You basically got an elephant-sized wallop of tranquilizer. Almost enough to stop your lungs."

At the mention of his lungs, Cody drew a deep full breath and began to feel more energetic. The sensations of his body were returning with a wave of warm tingles. He flexed his fingers and ankles, bent his knees. The more he breathed, the more he flexed, the easier it got.

"He's mad. In more ways than one," Cody said. And chuckled. Sara laughed with him. "How's Aisha?"

"She's good. She's right outside. I'm not letting her out of my sight. Between Achmed and those goons from the Vatican, we've got our hands full. Fortunately, there's some good news to go along with the bad. We've got a fix on Crimson Jihad. Or at least one of their operatives."

Cody's breathing was full and deep now. His hands were able to grasp the mattress. With some effort, he pushed himself to a sitting position. There. His legs buzzed with spasming tremors. It was starting to come back to him.

"Tell me," he said.

So Sara filled him in. She had studied the contents of Jacquard's zip drive. Several of the photos were of suspected CJ cell members, so she had enlisted Aisha to hack the city's CCTV system. The princess had proven as resourceful as she was resilient: after an afternoon's work, she had successfully tapped into the web of surveillance, traffic and public security cameras that connected digital Monte Carlo. Then Sara had arranged for Parsons to bit-torrent over a copy of the latest Vista-AI encrypted facial recognition software.

"We ran an algorithmic search laterally across the city's visual data banks. And we found one of them. He's here under forged papers, posing as a Palestinian guest worker. Jacquard's files suggest he may be part of a cell led by Selim Farah Mohammed."

"The White Wolf himself." Cody sighed as he maneuvered to a sitting position with his legs over the side of the bed. "If anyone is in the market for nukes, it's him. He spent a year in North Korea studying their nuclear program. He's been rumored to be the silent partner on a half-dozen yellowcake buys in the past decade. Where does our phony Palestinian work?"

"That's the best part." Sara produced her cellphone. "He's working in a sporting goods store. They move a lot of equipment around, including hunting and fishing gear. He's got a contact in construction. I'm thinking we should start there."

"They'll be making ready to move anything they acquire here down to safer shores in the Middle East. It's just a boat ride across the Med."

A knock came at the door and Aisha pushed in, cradling her laptop in her arms. She smiled warmly at Cody and moved beside him.

"It's good to see you back with us." She put a hand on his arm. "I hope my brother did not damage you too much?"

"I'm fine, thanks." Cody was glad to see her. "Sara tells me you've been a real help with the search. Thank you."

"You're welcome, Mr. Cody. And in fact I may have something more..."

Aisha set her laptop down on the wheeled bed table and turned the screen so they all could see.

"This vacant lot here..." She pointed at a Google Earth image. "It's a construction area. A helicopter comes in and out. Several other Middle Eastern men work there. I have traffic camera footage of the White Wolf's operative travelling there on successive days and meeting them. One day coincided with the helicopter's landing."

"So we've got their LZ. Nice work." Cody's voice held real approval. "What do we know about their chopper?"

Aisha swatted at the keyboard. As was common for commercial building sites, this one had its own CCTV system. She was able to pull up a still image of the aircraft from a camera that captured a profile view of the thing. She enlarged the image. Sara bent in and gave a low whistle.

"An Mi-24." Her voice held wonder. "Pretty slick how they've got her gussied up to resemble your basic civilian transport chopper, but I'd recognize that design anywhere. Saw them by the bushel in Syria."

Cody immediately recognized the distinctive Russian design, too. The 24 was a streamlined, all-purpose aircraft with a two-bubble cockpit and short stubby wing struts. Common since the 1970s in the Russian air arsenal, the chopper had also proven something of a cash cow for the Russian aeronautical industry. Many of the world's armed forces purchased the military version but the design was common enough to warrant a bestselling civilian model as well.

"Check out those engine baffles," he said, pointing. "To a civilian eye, just part of the fuselage. But those will conceal the standard suite of rocket launchers and gun mounts."

"Here." Her fingernail tapped the image. "Those ports? Normally where external machine guns go. But these round casters here could be flip ports. Maybe modified for short-barrel phalanx-style autocannons."

Cody nodded. "She can carry a payload of eight men. So there will be plenty of room in there to move equipment around from place to place. Aisha, you say this helicopter comes in on a regular schedule?"

"Yes. The White Wolf's man changed up his routine to visit the yard on that day. It's Thursday."

"Day after tomorrow," said Sara.

"So that's our next stake-out," he said. Grasping the side of the bed, he stood. Took several deep breaths. The dizziness he expected never came. "The trick now is to get close enough to Crimson Jihad so they'll lead us to Vetrov."

"It seems a dead certainty," agreed Sara.

"Crimson Jihad. Then Vetrov," said Cody mildly. "After that? We'll see."

# CHAPTER FIFTY

THE BUILDING SITE where Crimson Jihad was landing their chopper lay directly across the street from a multistory office complex. In the morning, Sara donned a bicycle messenger's get-up and did a walk-through. The third-floor suites overlooking the building site were occupied by a dentist's office that was open just three days per week.

"Should be easy to break into," she said upon return. "Simple slide-tongue lock, no alarm system. The floor itself is quiet. Looks like the lawyer next door often goes home after lunch. The offices across the way are empty."

"We'll go in at five," said Cody. "Just walk in the front door and take the elevator up to four. Walk down a flight. Aisha? You'll drive us. Then I want you to come back here and wait two hours before driving back. We'll coordinate by text so our exposure exiting is minimal. In and out. Got it?"

Aisha nodded.

The infiltration went perfectly. The street was quiet. Aisha pulled up smoothly to the curb. Cody and Sara alighted, walked in through the lobby, past the security guard at the reception desk and up the stairs to the third floor. When they entered through the fire doors, the echoing silence of the floor made it obvious they were alone. Sara crossed to the dentist's office and tried the door handle.

"This is the one," she said.

Cody moved in beside her with a strip of curved plastic that was flexible enough to curl around a door edge but tensile enough to hold the tongue of a lock still. He fed it in past the door frame, moving it up and down until the lock gave with an audible 'clack.' The door yawned open.

Beyond was a narrow waiting room and a glassed-in booth Cody guessed was used by the receptionist. Next to the booth was a doorway that led into a suite of examining rooms. Sara showed him the one that looked over the building site. Cody stepped over and looked down.

"It's big enough to land a chopper," he said. "I'm guessing Thursday is an early release day or some such. Our friends don't want the locals around rubbernecking."

"The profile is pretty low-key. No real lines of sight into the site except from here and that hotel over there."

Cody took the pair of field glasses she handed him and glassed the front of the hotel. He noticed a figure in a third-floor window, staring back at him.

A priest.

"Get down!"

The shotgun blast ripped through the office door. And then they were pouring in, a small team of around six men. Cody grabbed Sara and bolted into the furthest examining room. Outside the window was a fire escape.

"C'mon!" He locked the door - a futile gesture, but

better than nothing. It would buy them thirty seconds. He opened the window and stood aside as Sara climbed through. Raised voices crowded the corridor outside. The team was going from room to room. Cody slid out the window onto the fire escape just as the doorknob rattled.

"Let's go up," he said.

Sara took his meaning. Down was obvious. Any escaping quarry would opt for down. Only the supremely confident – or those supremely confident of back-up – went up. He followed Sara, who moved like a monkey, swinging from landing to stairs to landing with ease. Two flights and they reached the roof.

"Where to now?"

"Here." Cody knew there would be a roof access. And there was – a doorway isolated in a small triangular structure that concealed the first dozen steps of a stairwell. Cody ran over and tugged it open. The stairwell was clear.

"C'mon. We'll take it one floor at a time. They won't want to linger here."

"Agreed." She followed him onto the landing and they started down. They made it one floor before the priests found them.

The door burst open on the landing below and a man in black emerged, his sidearm in hand and held close to his body, combat style. He flicked his eyes first to the stairs heading down – a mistake which cost him. As he swept his eyes up, everything seemed to slow down...

He raised his head and turned it toward the stairs, eyes widening as he spotted Sara. He swung his gun arm toward them the instant after Sara's throwing knife dropped into her hand. With a flick of the wrist, it flew and lodged in the man's throat, killing him cleanly. He didn't make a sound, or even drop his gun when he fell.

Cody took the steps down to the body, bent and plucked at the man's collar. A strip of black cloth came away in his fingers. He held it up for Sara to see.

"They cover their priestly collars with this." Cody flapped the strip of cloth. "Clever. One moment, they're your friendly neighborhood priest. The next? They're Papal ninjas."

Voices rose from two landings below them. Working quickly, they opened the entrance to the floor, grasped the dead priest by his shoulders and succeeded in pulling him off the landing and closing the door behind them before the team below noticed. Cody straightened and looked around. He saw darkened offices, although some movement was visible behind the frosted glass of a door at the end of the hall. Fortunately, nobody had noticed their arrival.

Working quickly, Cody jimmied an office open, dragged the priest inside and shut the door behind them.

"Surprised that shotgun blast didn't summon the police," Sara said.

"It's on old building. Thick stone floors. All anyone heard was likely a muffled bang." Cody checked the load on his G1. Then he looked at his watch. "We have just over an hour until Aisha comes back. Chances are good that if we keep low, the team will miss us. I doubt they'll be entering locked offices."

"Too big a risk," Sara agreed. Then she pointed. "Right across the way. The windows in those rooms should look over the building site. We can finish our recon before we exfil."

"Sounds good." Cody dragged the body of the dead priest to an inner office, rolled him inside and shut the door. *Somebody's getting an unpleasant surprise when they show up at work in the morning,* he thought. Sara was standing by the hallway door when he returned, scanning the corridor.

"All quiet," she said. "I just heard them in the stairwell, heading down."

"They'll start at the bottom and go floor by floor," he said, pulling the plastic jimmy from his pocket. "I'll step out and get us into the office."

"Right behind you."

Cody slipped past her out the door. The corridor was dark and quiet. Two steps and he was at the entrance to the office across the hall. The sign identified it as an insurance broker as near as he could tell. It was dark beyond the frosted glass in the door. Cody glanced left and right before sliding the plastic wedge between the door and jamb. The lock mechanism was old and fussy. It took a little extra time, but he managed to open the office just as the elevator door parted. He ducked inside just before a janitor appeared, pushing a broom cart. Cody waited until the janitor entered the washroom before opening the door and beckoning Sara across.

Dusk fell as they stood at the windows overlooking the construction yard. Footsteps, then the wheeled cart of the passing janitor sounded in the corridor outside. Sara had turned on the vestibule lights behind the locked door to discourage the cleaner. If any of the footsteps belonged to the Vatican hit team, they never bothered trying the door.

"The priests will be under orders to keep a low profile," Sara muttered, checking her watch. "We've got about forty-five minutes left."

Cody glassed the empty construction yard one last time before lowering the binoculars. Aside from assessing the entry and exit points and measuring the size of the site, their recon had yielded very little actionable intelligence. Before full darkness fell, Cody pointed out a gate on the far side of the yard.

"We'll go in there tomorrow," he told Sara. "Slip in right after closing time."

"They finish early on Thursdays, according to Jacquard's notes."

"Okay. Should be fairly straightforward. We'll go in and wait -"

She grasped his arm and pointed. "Look!"

Cody raised the binoculars. There, in the glow of headlights from a car parked by the construction yard fence, stood Vetrov.

# CHAPTER FIFTY-ONE

"IT'S HIM, ALRIGHT." Cody's tone was grim. Every muscle and nerve in his body yearned to smash a hole in the window and put a bullet in the guy.

*One step at a time,* he reminded himself. Their first task was to locate and secure the nukes.

"There." Sara touched his arm. "That's our guy. The one from Jacquard's files."

Cody adjusted the angle of his binoculars. The twin circles swished left, then right over a blur of blackness and lights until they settled on a hunched figure approaching Vetrov along the sidewalk. When he paused and turned his face up into the light, Cody recognized him as the 'Palestinian' representative of the White Wolf. He watched as the man sidled up to Vetrov and pretended to ask for a light.

"They're playing it close to the chest," he muttered.

"We're coming down to it," Sara said, holding up her watch. "Aisha will be here in fifteen."

"Text her and tell her to wait around the corner until we give the all-clear." He gestured with the binoculars.

"Seems we've finally got all the pieces lined up. Missing nukes. Vetrov. Now Crimson Jihad. Product, thief and customer. How much you want to bet they plan to do the exchange here tomorrow?"

"If I was a betting woman, I might take you up on that." Her words softened around a smile and he felt her hand on the small of his back. "But I only bet on sure things."

He turned and met her gaze. They held each other's eyes for a long moment before she broke away to fire off a text to Aisha.

*So what's the plan?* Cody wondered. He swished the binocs from Vetrov and the 'Palestinian' to glass the yard and the airspace above it. It was a narrow approach, but there was plenty of room to land a chopper on the site. Thirty Hummingbird portable nukes was a considerable payload, but not too bulky for a regular-sized van. The site was closed off by tall wooden barricades into which a fence opening had been built. *There,* he thought. They'll land the chopper, bring in a van, offload and then go their separate ways.

"They can probably do the entire drop-off and transfer within fifteen minutes," he said. "Less if the chopper is left idling."

"So what's the plan?"

"We stop him cold. Ambush the meet. Stop the transfer. Neutralize Vetrov. And Thelma Justice if she's there, too."

Sara's cellphone wheeped. She checked the screen. "Aisha's in-bound."

Down in the street, Vetrov and his crony were parting company. As Cody watched, the terrorist crossed the street and vanished while Vetrov climbed into his car.

"Okay. Let's go."

They let themselves out into the hallway. The entire floor was dark by now, and the janitor was long gone. They opted for the elevator as the least inconspicuous route. An empty car arrived soon after Sara punched the down button. A quick, quiet ride brought them to the lobby where they stepped out into half-light.

"They really roll up the sidewalks around here," observed Sara, casting around. The building was obviously closed, the only presence a night watchman reading a newspaper at a desk by the door.

"ALL CLEAR," muttered Cody. Aisha pulled up outside. "There's our ride."

They started across the lobby. Cody kept his guard up, scanning left and right. Nobody at the entrance and nobody on the sidewalks. Everything looked good ...

Out of instinct, he glanced over his shoulder.

The priest emerged from the shadows by the first-floor washroom. Cody grabbed Sara's shoulder and pushed her down just as the man raised his machine-pistol and fired. A spray of bullets washed the room, smashing furniture and glass and startling the security guard behind the desk, who hit the deck.

Cody and Sara drew their own sidearms and returned fire. The priest ducked back into the washroom.

"I got this," she said. Cody covered her as she crouched and moved forward, hugging the walls. She reached the wall by the men's room door as the priest peeped out. He didn't see her. Cody drove the man back inside with a few well-placed shots. After he took refuge, Cody gave Sara the high-sign and waited.

She reached into a pocket of her jacket and withdrew a small cannister. Pushing a button on the top, kicked open the bathroom door and tossed it inside, taking refuge from the answer volley of gunfire. A moment later, the door pulsed as a dull explosion rocked the lavatory. Smoke from the flash-bang leaked into the shattered lobby. Then Sara was kicking open the door and bathing the tiled bathroom in a storm of bullets.

Cody turned. The night watchman's chair was empty, his newspaper abandoned on the desk. As Cody noticed this, the night watchman poked his head up over the edge of the desk and pointed tentatively at the phone.

*"LA POLICE?"* he asked timidly.

Cody shook his head. *"C'est pas necessaire,"* said Sara, reloading. Then she holstered her sidearm and she and Cody moved onto the sidewalk. Aisha glided up to the curb. They got in and soon melted into the evening traffic.

———

UPON RETURN to Jacquard's cottage, Cody and Sara sank into chairs at the kitchen table, exhausted. Aisha joined them, taking a seat at the place where her laptop sat open. Judging from the notes jotted on the pad next to her in pencil, she had been working on something.

"This Vatican team has a long reach." Cody stared at Aisha for a long moment. Then he pulled the G1 from its holster, unloaded and began disassembling it for cleaning, talking as he worked. "They rumbled Jacquard, got a fix on his operation, were even able to locate one of his store of stashed vehicles."

"And blow it to Kingdom Come." Sara tilted back in

her chair and stared up at the ceiling. "How long until they find this place?"

"They won't," said Aisha abruptly.

Cody and Sara turned to her.

"Jacquard concealed his ownership of this place very carefully." Aisha flipped a few pages in her notebook until she found a folded sheet and produced it. "I found this. It's the deed to the house. It's in the name of a blind trust. And according to city records, this place is currently unowned and not on the market."

"Smart," said Sara. "Jacquard created his own safe-house for refuge. He must have known enemies were watching him."

"So we have some time to plan and assess." Cody stood and pulled a bottle of gun oil down from a kitchen shelf. "Tomorrow night, that chopper comes down in the construction zone. And we'll be there to intercept what-ever Vetrov has planned."

"It could be," Aisha said, "that the transfer won't be taking place there. In fact, I would bet on it."

"Why?" asked Sara.

Aisha turned her laptop so both of them could see the screen. "I've been studying the building site," she said. "There are CCTV cameras on the streets and busi-nesses around it. With Monsieur Jacquard's crypto key, I've been able to slip in and access their file storage..."

"Nice work," muttered Cody.

"... and cross-reference it with this." Aisha clicked the mouse and a second screen appeared – a city map of Monte Carlo overlaid with sets of green arrows. "French air traffic diagrams."

Sara sat forward, peering at the screen. "Of course," she marveled. "Why not? It's a 'hide-in-plain-sight' type arrangement. The flight would be tracked by civilian radar."

"I have compared footage and radar records for the past three weeks and overlaid them on this map of the city." She brought up the image. "It's tied into Google Earth. Notice something?"

Cody sat forward over the parts of his disassembled gun. "All three are heading in the same direction."

Aisha nodded and clicked the mouse again. A set of red arrows appeared, projecting the likely course of the chopper's flight. "All three flights are directly on course to end ... here."

A red arrow winked into visibility on screen. Aisha double-clicked on it and an aerial image of Thelma Justice's compound appeared.

Cody and Sara sat in silence for a long moment. At length, she spoke.

"There it is," she said quietly. "Vetrov, Thelma Justice, the transfer... all tied together right there."

"If you intercept that flight tomorrow, you could end this all in one stroke," said Aisha.

"Intercept. Or commandeer," said Cody. "One swift stroke and we can cut the snake's head off. And that's what we plan to do."

# CHAPTER FIFTY-TWO

THEY NO LONGER HAD JACQUARD, or any of his resources with the police or French intelligence. So they made do with what was available.

Aisha had impressed Cody with her computer skills and resourcefulness, so they converted the kitchen into an ad-hoc logistics center. Using Jacquard's encryption tool, they infiltrated every public and private CCTV network they found that was in close proximity to the building site. Then they downloaded some shareware that enabled her to track civilian flight traffic over the city.

"Princess, you'll remain here in the cottage." Cody adjusted the fit of his shoulder holster and checked the load on the G1. "Your job will be to relay Sara and I intel on the chopper's approach and any personnel you see moving on or around the building site by CCTV. You'll be our eyes and ears."

"Cody and I will feed intel back to you from the ground," Sara said. "That's the way it's done in our line of work. It's a feedback loop. That way we all have a clear picture of the total situation at any given moment."

Jacquard had equipped them with a set of encrypted radios. Sara and Cody each took one and left a third on the table beside Aisha's computer.

"Redundancy of comms," Cody said. "Radios on A frequency. Fallback frequency is B. If the radios are out, we'll go to cellphones."

"Got it," said Aisha.

"If worse comes to worse and somebody rumbles this place..." Sara pointed to the back door. "Grab the laptop and radio and head out the back. We'll rendezvous two blocks from here in front of the supermarket."

The girl nodded.

"Okay." Cody holstered his pistol. "Game time."

———

THEY SAT TOGETHER in a car across the street from the construction site, watching the workers depart for the day. In ones and twos, lunchboxes and hard-hats in hand, they tumbled out through the gate in the wooden fence, some making for cars, others for busses or bars while still others clustered in small groups to smoke cigarettes and bitch about work. *Similar scenes occur,* Cody reflected, *at construction sites all over the world. Everyone is in a hurry to get home at the end of the work day...*

"There," said Sara. "Look."

A man alighted from a passenger bus just as a clutch of construction workers were climbing aboard. Cody recognized the 'Palestinian' operative immediately. He drifted along the sidewalk in a leisurely fashion, blending in with the workers. He nodded and spoke to a few as he lingered around the entrance gate. As the last few workers departed, he slipped onto the building site while the foreman's back was turned.

"The old porta-potty trick," Sara chuckled. "Is he really that basic?"

"Apparently," said Cody. Sure enough, the man approached one of the portable toilets on site, stepped inside and closed the door. He remained there for twenty minutes. When the foreman did a final sweep of the site, he didn't check the porta-potties. Taking up his own lunchbox, he pulled shut the gate, conferred briefly with one of the workers on the sidewalk and then made for his car.

Sara thumbed her radio mike. "Aisha? You have eyes on the site?"

"Aisha here. I do," came the reply. "That one fellow is still in the washroom."

"Confirmed." Sara turned to Cody. "So far, we're on track."

"How long until the chopper's usual arrival time?"

She checked her watch. "Another ten minutes."

Right on schedule, ten minutes later, Aisha's voice came over the radio:

"I have a single flight, low over the city, heading in your direction," she intoned. "It fits the profile of the helicopter."

"Okay," said Cody. He winked at Sara. "See you on the other side."

"Be careful," she said, and stole a quick kiss.

Cody let himself out and crossed the street. He went to the corner and made a right, circling around to the gate at the rear of the building site. The gate was in a narrow alley that provided access to the backlots and rear entrances of the businesses and apartment buildings of two blocks. Cody approached the mesh gate and peered through. Not a soul in sight. The gate was secured by a simple padlock.

Working quickly, Cody removed a lockpick from his pocket and attacked the padlock. The tumblers were easy enough to find but the lock was old, rusted, making the work more difficult than it had to be. By the time Cody was done, the thrumming of the helicopter could be heard approaching from a distance. Aisha's voice sounded in his ear:

"Chopper inbound. Estimating time of arrival in three minutes."

Cody unpinned the lock, parted the mesh fence and moved onto the site. He closed and dummy-locked the fence behind him, taking refuge behind a pile of lumber as the 'Palestinian' let himself out of the porta-potty. Cody watched as the man cast a careful eye over the area, going the extra mile to make sure he was alone. Satisfied, he turned and headed into the office trailer.

CODY WAITED. The thrumming of the chopper grew deafening. The 'Palestinian' was gone for a good long while. He emerged as the chopper appeared overhead and began its descent, a steel briefcase in hand.

# CHAPTER FIFTY-THREE

SARA, still behind the wheel of the car, watched the chopper begin its descent from across the street. From below, the Mi-24 cut a distinct silhouette in the darkening sky. She scanned the underside, noting several shapes that could easily be armaments emplacements. As she did, she reflected that the spectre of a '24 lowering itself toward the ground was probably the last thing a great many enemies of Russia had seen in their lives.

The pilot of the chopper switched on a spotlight. The construction yard became bathed in brilliance. Had she been piloting the craft herself, Sara would have preferred more clearance between the buildings on either side. But whoever was behind the stick knew what they were doing.

Checking to see that the sidewalks were clear, she let herself out as the chopper reached fence-top level. Because of the tall building on either side of the lot, the prop wash created a wind trap, forcing dirt and dust straight upwards into the sky. Glancing both ways, she crossed the street, reaching the main gate as the din of the chopper reached its loudest.

Working quickly, she picked the padlock and cracked open the wooden barrier. The 'Palestinian' stood a hundred yards away, his back to her, watching the aircraft descend. Sara chose that moment to sneak inside, closing the gate behind her. She ducked behind the office trailer and drew her pistol.

For a minute, the construction lot became the epicenter of a sandstorm as the 24 finished its descent. It touched down, bouncing on its wheels. The pilot extinguished the spotlight and switched on the exterior lights. They were enough to send shafts of brilliance into the now-darkened yard. The propellers slowed, finally coming to a complete stop. The hatch opened and the pilot emerged.

Sara shouldn't have been surprised it was a woman, but she was. But this was no Middle Easterner. Lithe and athletic, the pilot wore her blond hair in a butch trim and wore a flight-suit Sara recognized as Russian in design. She guessed this would be one of Vetrov's close confederates.

The 'Palestinian' approached, carrying the case in his hands. He and the woman greeted each other. They spoke Arabic, the man in smooth, easy tones and the woman in clipped, clumsy phrases, leaning on the vowels as a Russian would. Sara noted the pilot's military bearing, her watchfulness and the sidearm holstered at her belt. *Russian military, no doubt,* she thought. As she did, the 'Palestinian' lifted the item in his hands and placed it on the edge of the hatch.

*Hummingbird,* she realized, a hot flush of worry prickling the back of her skull. She recognized the unit from briefings she had received at Langley. To an untrained eye, the suitcase nuke resembled a piece of tourist luggage. But the triple padlocks, the handcuff anchor and the slight flange at the base of the item gave it away for what it was.

The man spun the padlocks, flipped the catches and raised the lid. The pilot stepped over, scanned the array of electronics in the interior and nodded.

*The question now,* Sara thought, *is whether that's a sample or the first of the shipment.*

She soon had her answer. The pilot moved away, the man closed the case and made ready to board the chopper with it. The pilot began circling the hull in her pre-flight check.

Sara slipped around the back of the office trailer and began to approach the chopper from behind.

It was go-time.

# CHAPTER FIFTY-FOUR

CODY SAW the pilot begin to circle the chopper. Any moment now she would be in line-of-sight. He took the opportunity to change position, remaining close to the fence, concealed by piles of equipment and parked vehicles. He saw Sara across the yard, closing in on the pilot. They shared a nod before each falling to their separate tasks.

Cody came around to the front of the chopper. The 'Palestinian' terrorist was standing by the hatch, securing the Hummingbird to the floor of the chopper with bungie cords.

It was now or never.

Cody edged out of the shadows, approaching the man from behind. It was a short distance. Seventy yards. Fifty. Forty. Then...

The man turned and saw Cody barreling down on him. He opened his mouth to shout a warning but by then Cody was on top of him, grabbing him by the lapels and bending him backwards over the edge of the chopper hatch. The man gasped, moaning with the pain, trying to gather enough wind to holler. But Cody's stress hold made that impossible.

The terrorist unwrapped one hand from around Cody's wrist and began scrabbling at his clothes. Cody's priorities went from 'capture' to 'kill.' He plunged forward with one hand, wrapping the tips of his fingers around the larynx and tightening. The man's eyes went wide. Then his hand came out from under his clothes holding a knife.

Cody had to release and dodge back in order to avoid the point. The man advanced, teeth bared, no longer keen to warn the pilot. He would close the distance. He would do away with this infidel interloper. Cody thought of reaching for his gun but knew the sound of the shot would alert the pilot. And so he assumed a defensive stance and waited.

THE POINT of the knife was a glimmering firefly in the semi-dark. It was in the man's right hand, then his left. When he struck, the 'Palestinian' did so laterally, sweeping the air before him in a broad oval. Cody waited until the point of the blade whipped by, then came in low with a football tackle. The rush connected, the man was driven back and the breath smashed from his lungs when he connected with the side of the chopper. Then he was moving again.

The knife was a living thing, twisting and plunging through the air like a snake. It was gripped in the man's right fist, point downward, and Cody's hand was wrapped around the man's wrist. He was strong. He put the power of his shoulder behind each swipe of the blade but Cody's strength kept the point at bay. The man was trapped, bent backward into the chopper over the edge of the hatch, panicking and running out of breath. Cody's hand went back to the man's throat...

Then the man drove upward with his knee, aiming for Cody's testicles. He missed but managed to slam the inside of Cody's thigh, which was painful enough. Cody stumbled, falling back, and the man gathered enough air in his lungs to scream:

*"Natalya!"*

Cody shot him.

———

SARA WATCHED the pilot approach the back of the chopper for her pre-flight check. Sara appraised her opponent. The woman was the same size as her and moved with the sinewy ease of a trained fighter. This would have to be quiet so as not to alert the 'Palestinian.' Sara holstered her sidearm, flexed her hands and waited.

THE PILOT SLOWED as she approached the tail section. Something had evidently caught her eye. She stepped toward the fuselage and opened a small port in the tail to check the equipment inside. She craned up on her tiptoes, pushing her nose toward the electronics. Sara slipped out and began her approach from behind.

The pilot was too absorbed to notice. The sound of the traffic on the street outside abruptly rose, providing Sara with some fortuitous sound cover...

"Natalya!"

The pilot snapped her head around in time to see Sara closing on her. She spun and brought up her hands just as Sara lashed out with a kick that connected solidly with the pilot's solar plexus. The woman bent double and fell to her knees...

A gunshot.

Sara moved on the pilot, fist clenched, one hand out to grab her hair. Suddenly, the pilot was lunging, hands wrapping Sara's knees and pulling her legs out from under her. With a crash, the pilot came down on top and the two grappled for a moment. When Sara's hand flashed within reach of her mouth, the pilot grasped it in her teeth and bit down hard enough to draw blood.

As Sara drew back, the pilot rolled, trapping Sara under her. She reached for her sidearm ...

A second gunshot and she slumped to the ground, lifeless.

Sara looked up.

Cody knelt a short distance away, both hands to his still-smoking pistol. Beyond lay the body of the Syrian. Sara released a breath and sat up, shaking her head. From a distance came the wail of sirens. The sound of two gunshots in the middle of downtown Monte Carlo was sufficiently unusual to raise an alarm.

"You okay?" he asked.

"Yeah." She stood. "I'm thinking it's time we split."

The sound of the sirens grew deafening and Cody could see the first traces of red light flickering close.

"Yeah," he said. He holstered the G1. "Let's go."

They made for the chopper's hatch.

# CHAPTER FIFTY-FIVE

CODY PULLED the hatch shut as Sara took a seat in the pilot's chair. Hands moving smoothly over the controls, she brought the power online and coaxed the rotors into sluggish motion. The Mi-24 was surprisingly responsive. By the time Cody strapped himself in, the blades were starting to whip around, lashing bits of paper and debris up from the ground of the construction yard. He checked the window. In the glow of a running light, he could just make out the leg of the dead Syrian where he lay.

"Pretty standard console," Sara said, casting an eye over the controls labelled in Cyrillic. She reached up and flicked a few ceiling toggles. "Should be able to get us aloft here in just a minute..."

The street before the construction yard was now awash in a sea of red lights. The local cops had responded in force. They would soon be through the gate.

"Where to, captain?" he asked.

She shrugged. "I thought we might stick with the original flight plan."

"You know what that is?"

She held up a folded sheaf of papers. "Maps don't lie."

Cody examined the map in the dim light. Scrawled in red ink were a series of arrows ending at a circled X. "Thelma Justice's compound," he said quietly. "There's nothing else out that way."

"That's our next stop," she said. Overhead, the sound of the rotors had risen to a shriek. "Ready?"

The gate burst open, the first of the French cops entering, gun drawn.

"Let's go," she said.

She grasped the stick. The French cop was waving his arms. When he saw they would not stop, he levelled his gun and fired. The bullet whined off of the shielded cockpit glass. Sara punched a button and, with a whine of turbines, the chopper began to rise. The construction zone floated away beneath them as they climbed, gunfire chasing them into the sky. Soon, the city was a puddle of lights far below.

"So Vetrov will be waiting," Cody said. "And the nukes will be there with him, or somewhere close by. Probably a reception committee, too."

"They better be strapped." Sara passed a hand over the weapons station. "This bad boy is armed to the teeth. It's got a Yak Gatling gun set-up. Looks to be almost 2000 rounds of ammo. Two autocannons and it looks like... yeah. We've got wing-mounted rocket launchers."

"Christmas came early."

"So it would seem." She fixed him with a serious stare. "So, what's your plan? There's just two of us. It's not like we can go full Entebbe with this raid."

"I'm thinking I'll handle Vetrov. You handle everyone else."

"Alone?"

"Nah. Here in your new toy."

"New toy is right." She grinned. "Wouldn't mind having one of these back home. Damned if I know where I'd park it, though..."

"That might be tough in DC," he admitted.

The countryside passed below them, a yawning blackness that began where the lights of town faded out. At this elevation, the glow of Thelma Justice's estate was visible in the distance. It would be a short flight.

"Not sure what their schedule is for an RV," Cody said. "But I'm thinking if we arrive a few minutes late, it shouldn't be that big a deal..."

"What do you have in mind?"

"We've got some good optics gear back there." He hooked a thumb over his shoulder. "If you climb to ceiling and do a few circles over the compound, we can get a sense of what we're walking into."

"Good idea." She adjusted the controls and the 24 began to climb. She was an incredibly responsive craft – so much so that Sara had to adjust the pitch to ensure they didn't climb nose-first like an airplane. She brought them up a bit at a time, maintaining a horizontal attitude as Cody moved to the gunner station and began hotting up the night vision gear.

Designed as a multi-purpose combat aircraft, the Mi-24 could fly, ferry troops or fight if necessary. Night vision accessories were absolutely essential for a door gunner in modern warfare and Cody could tell the owners of this craft had spared no expense. The make of the UV vision gear was unfamiliar to Cody but the set-up was pretty intuitive. He donned the heavy goggles, securing them in place with a head strap before touching the power button. The landscape below exploded in green and black before his eyes.

"I've got night vision," he told Sara over the headset radio.

"Beginning recon run now," she replied, her voice crisp over the connection.

Below, the dark countryside gave way to a lit circle against the black. Thelma Justice's compound was as Cody remembered – the main house, the admin facility and the rows of Quonset huts marching toward the back fence. But his alarm bells went off the moment he recognized what was amiss down there.

"We have zero movement," he reported. "Not a soul visible on the ground. No vehicles. No people. No nothing."

"They must have got word about downtown."

"Agreed. They're either hunkered down or gone."

"So what do you think?"

Cody pondered for a moment. "I say we continue as normal. Pretend nothing has happened. See what happens when we land."

"Recon anyway. That's good." Sara made an adjustment and they began descending. "If they're gone we'll do a sweep of the facility and see what we can find."

"Okay. Let's do it."

Cody returned to the cockpit. Sara executed a maneuver that steered the chopper in toward the compound as if from town. A thousand feet out, she switched on the spotlight. It knifed through the dark to the helicopter pad. In the white-hot oval of its glare, Cody saw the circle with the cross at its center, the windsock hanging limp on its pole and the waist-high gate surrounding the landing pad. But no trace of a reception committee.

"There." He pointed. "Get me a look at the main house, would you?"

"Roger." Sara twisted the knob that controlled the directional spotlight. The light crawled over the darkened facade and windows. There was no sign of anyone on the porch or within. She conducted a similar sweep around the landing zone. There wasn't a soul to be seen.

"Bring her in," said Cody. "Land, cut power and go dark. I'll slip out the hatch. You stay put. Once I'm out of sight, power up and prep for a fast dust-off."

"Will do."

Sara lowered the chopper the last hundred feet. The 24 touched down with a gentle bump of its rubber wheels. The moment they connected, Sara killed the lights and Cody shouldered open the hatch, hit the ground, rolled and came up in a crouch, gun held in a two-handed grip.

# CHAPTER FIFTY-SIX

SILENCE. Stillness.

Nothing.

Cody came to his feet and looked over the shoulder. The chopper was a dark shape behind him. Remaining low, he moved toward the fence, scanning left and right through the G1's sights. There was a tight knot at the back of his neck and his spine was tense in anticipation of a bullet. But by the time he climbed over the fence it was obvious no reception committee awaited them.

*If Vetrov is here he's probably staying in the house,* he thought. Cody made his way in that direction, weapon first, his every sense alert for signs of danger.

His worst nightmare in night combat was the possibility of a concealed sniper. He had lost two colleagues in Lebanon to a terrorist sniper concealed in a third-floor apartment. By the time his team crashed in to exact vengeance, the man was already dead, killed by a stray bullet during the infiltration. But Cody had been impressed by the rig he had. High-end rifles were available for purchase on the internet by anyone with enough money, and Cody's sniper had kitted his out with a night-vision scope stolen from the IDF. That set-up had ended the lives of two special forces soldiers.

*Probably didn't cost him more than four grand to put that all together,* Cody thought. And the thought sobered him as he continued to press forward. The dark facade of the house was two hundred yards away, one-fifty, one hundred ... And then Cody was flattening himself against the wall, his eyes probing the windows for any sign of light or drawn curtains. But again: nothing.

The front door was open.

HAD Thelma's organization pulled another vanishing act like Moscow? It was possible. Perhaps the plan was just to rendezvous here, not load the Hummingbirds out of the house into the chopper. Were the nukes en route? That was possible, too. But Cody wouldn't get any answers standing here. Raising his gun again, he moved toward the door.

————

SARA, too, felt unnerved by the silence. What was going on? Could it be that she'd misread the flight plan? But when she double-checked, she discovered that she had not. The longer she watched Cody cross the grounds and enter the main house unchallenged, the more convinced she became that something wasn't right.

Her hands fell to the control console. The Russian chopper, despite its civilian camouflage, was still very much a war bird. All the toys and tech one might expect from an operational combat aircraft were present. Although she couldn't read the Cyrillic lettering, she knew what she was looking at. The Mi-24 came equipped with a computerized weapons system, a split-screen windshield/data display, radar-guided targeting package and infra-vision capability. This last enabled the gunship operators to detect human heat signatures - even those of enemies sheltering under the trees or within buildings.

Cody was safely inside now. She re-activated the main systems console and ran through a pre-flight check. Seeing everything was five-by-five, she primed the rotors and set them on slow, pre-take-off revolutions. Then she returned her attention to the infra-vision panel.

Ordinarily, a Russian pilot would be wearing a smart helmet with data ports he could just plug in to access optics systems. But there was a redundancy set of goggles hard-wired into the system hanging just above the pilot's chair. She drew these down now, activated the infra-vision subroutine and began scanning the property.

*Oh my god...*

Bunched around the base of the office complex and Quonset huts, hugging the walls, were a blur of heat signatures. Thelma Justice had her men out in force, lying in wait to spring an ambush.

She was so deeply immersed she did not see the dark shape emerge out of the shadows and dash below the helicopter's fuselage.

———

CODY EDGED FORWARD into the vestibule, gun up, hugging the wall. There was still furniture present, artwork hanging on the walls and he could tell from the glow of the alarm panel that the electricity was still hooked up. If this was a vanishing act, it was a marvel of shoddy execution.

He conducted a sweep of the immediate area: entry-way, living room, the short hallway leading to the kitchen. A row of windows over the stove threw light on floor and countertops. Cody ghosted through the room, keeping to the shadows. Pausing, he eased open a drawer and looked inside. Light glimmered off of silver cutlery. There were pans and plates in the cabinets above. So the silence was not due to a bug-out operation.

He was very conscious of burning daylight. Only another few minutes, then he would have to backtrack to the chopper and figure out next steps. But he did have one more avenue to try.

He dug in a pocket and found his cellphone. Touching the screen, he scrolled until finding the icon for an app called Geiger_(f)Lash. Two taps and it came active. The cellphone's screen transformed into a Geiger counter. As Cody retraced his steps, he swept the phone back and forth in front of him. The digital read-out remained at 00.00.00 until he reached the living room. Then the numbers began climbing ...

00.00.01 ... 00.00.05 ... 00.02.75 ... 00.83.77 ...

There was definitely something in the house emitting a high-saturation radiological signature. The signal-to-noise ratio on the Geiger display rose the closer he came to the entry hall. Then it dropped off abruptly. He retraced his steps. The signal peaked at a narrow door-way. Cody eased it open. A flight of stairs led downward.

The phone held out before him, he began to descend.

# CHAPTER FIFTY-SEVEN

SARA GAVE one more quick glance to the console readings before rising from the pilot's chair and heading aft. Cody had told her to be ready for a quick dust-off, so the last thing she had to do was a pre-flight walk-around. Easing open the hatch, she jumped down, straightened and then began her inspection.

It lasted six steps. She was aware of the presence - a shadow skulking below the fuselage - a bare second before it struck.

A crunch of gravel. A footstep behind her. Sara's evasion/escape training kicked in and she dropped low. Standard CIA practice when someone sneaks up from behind: most such assailants come in with the confidence to strike high on the body and this one was no different. Sara saw a knife swish through the air above her. Then she tripoded - two hands and one foot, sweeping out with the other leg.

She hit the Fury at calf-level. The woman soldier fell, her knife clattering away in the dark, before Sara came down on top of her. They struck at each other, punching and blocking punches, Sara seeking to bring her knees to the ground on either side of her opponent and the woman below bridging and rolling, looking for an escape. She succeeded just as Sara wrapped her hands around the woman's windpipe.

*Damn, this one knows jiu-jitsu,* Sara thought angrily as she lost her grip and crashed to the ground.

Now it was the Fury's turn to go on the attack. She balled up a fist and hit Sara hard in the face - hard enough to leave bruises. Sara gritted her teeth, tasting blood, arms coming together to cover her face. The Fury was tugging at one arm, seeking to isolate and break it.

SHE'S GOOD, Sara thought. Probably a black belt. She knew when she was outclassed. So she did the unexpected.

When the woman's forearm came within reach, Sara bared her teeth. With a desperation born of fear, she grasped a hunk of flesh between her incisors and bit down harder than she ever had in her life. The Fury howled above her, all the strategic calm so patiently drilled into her on the mats crumbling in the face of Sara's primal attack. She flinched back, but not before Sara's hands came up and gripped her face.

The woman jerked and wobbled, unable to break away. That's when Sara worked a fingernail into position and ripped the woman's left eye out of its socket.

The Fury reared back and howled. She started raising one hand to her face before stopping suddenly and yanking it back in disgust. She did *not* want to encounter that knobby bulb of flesh hanging at the end of a head-spaghetti tendon! Next, she was up and fleeing. She ran directly into the side of the chopper and rebounded. Right onto the point of Sara's blade.

———

CODY REACHED the bottom of the stairs and paused. He had emerged into a wide, long concrete tunnel inset with overhead lights and air vents. It was the sort of tunnel Cody recalled seeing when he'd visited the Cheyenne Mountain complex, home of the US Strategic Air Command. The Feds had spent a small fortune creating the underground city that housed the command-and-control complex of the American nuclear defense deterrent. Thelma Justice appeared to have also spent some money - more than the average homeowner.

*Looks like a fancy air raid shelter,* he thought. The construction quality and the reinforced concrete finish suggested the kind of effort put into protecting something vitally important. Something... or someone.

Cody took once last glance at the read-out, then switched off his phone. The sequence of bulbs running along the ceiling had been dimmed to every other one. He allowed his eyes to adjust to the semi-dark. The Geiger readings were off the chart heading in this direction. Now was the time to move it along smartly, finish the recon and get back to Sara.

The corridor stretched on for one hundred yards before an opening appeared in the right-hand wall. A dim spill of light painted the floor, emanating from within. Cody sidled up to the open doorway and peered around.

At one time, it had obviously served as some sort of workshop or repair bay. A thick-hewn workbench stood across from the door, a large vise balanced at its far edge.

Racks of tools lined the wall above. Beyond were the dim suggestions of lifts and pressure tools - the sort of set-up you might see in an automotive repair shop. Whoever ran this place was nowhere in sight, but the results of his work were plain to see.

Scattered across the floor and workbench were numerous stainless steel briefcases - thirty in all, to be exact. And every single one had been opened and its contents removed, leaving behind only the Humming-bird's harmless camouflage shell. The nukes had been carefully removed, stripped out of their cocoons and put...

*Where?*

Cody opted to take a chance. One quick sweep of the room would tell him much about where the warheads had gone. He reactivated his Geiger app. The reading jumped off the scale before settling down to a constant low simmer. He edged across the floor toward the nearest open case. The remains of the Hummingbird lay on its back, edges poking the air like a beetle over-turned on its shell. The Geiger reading jumped with each step closer. He held the cellphone higher. The combined reading from all of them was...

He heard the snap of a bullet being chambered somewhere behind him. Sighing, he raised his hands and turned slowly until he was face to face with Vetrov.

"I knew eventually you would find your way," the Russian admitted icily. "Smart Yankee boy. Is easier to hide from Russian intelligence than from you. Difference is... they are not crazy. Like you. Cody. Suicide Cody."

"Yeah, that's right." Cody smiled broadly. "It's awfully inconvenient for you, I get that. Not having an enemy you can scare, I mean. That's got to be frustrating as hell for a guy like you. How the hell do you cope?"

"Listen to me." Vetrov sounded exasperated. "Every army, every force has man like you. Over-performer. Superstar who encounter sudden tragedy, yes? Like wife and kid killed by bomb. Boom. There go your life, your career. Confidence shattered, no?"

"No." Cody spoke softly. "Confidence replaced. By yearning."

"For?"

"The end." Cody's voice was a disembodied whisper. "Show respect, general. Death is in the room."

For a second, Vetrov seemed to waver. "Any moment, death come for your friend. We hear in advance about hit at construction yard. Our forces here, concealed, awaiting your arrival. Soon they -"

But his voice was drowned out by the sound of a sudden explosion from above.

# CHAPTER FIFTY-EIGHT

SARA CAUGHT the dead Fury's body as she fell and eased it to the ground. All around her, silence deepened. The night was still - so still it was unsettling. She felt the eyes out there. She felt the tense anticipation of violence, contained. She knew what was coming. Even before it came.

Lights: one... two... three. They came on, one after another, bathing the landing pad and surrounding area in a corona of light. Then she was twisting on one heel and sprinting for the hatch. The silhouettes of the figures she saw approaching - dozens of them - carried automatic weapons. She could hear the sound of weapons being locked and loaded as she ducked inside. Then she was closing the hatch and sprinting forward.

The first volley of machine-gun fire hit right as she took the pilot's chair. It ripped across the armored glass of the fuselage, leaving streaks but doing no damage. Another spray went wide. Sara sat, kicked the rotors from their lazy twirl into a furious chop. Then she turned to the weapons console. Fingers dancing across its fire control panel, she heated up the Yak.

If there was any one area of engineering in which the Russian mind excelled, it was in armaments. The Yaku-shev-Borzov ('Yak' for short) was one such marvel of sinister design. The four-barrel, rotary-canon weapon was capable of delivering 4 - 5,000 rounds of 12.7 mm ammo per minute. This beast was mounted on an under-nose turret that growled and came to life at Sara's touch. Abruptly, it swiveled toward the line of attackers and roared to life.

Tracers shredded the ranks. The Yak, designed for both air-to-air and air-to-ground combat, was designed to render vehicles and aircraft inoperable. They had little difficulty turning the Furies of Harmony into so much shredded beef.

BY NOW, the rotors were whirling. Sara grasped the stick and began to ease the ship up from her moorings. The Mi-24 rose grudgingly, its rotors kicking up a storm of dust and complaint. Sara was set to elevate the pitch and climb higher when something outside caught her attention. Two of the Furies were kneeling and moving something into position. It took her a moment to recognize...

*Shoulder-fired missile!*

She peeled away moments before the rocket struck the landing pad, reducing it to rubble.

———

VETROV SPUN TOWARD THE EXPLOSION, his gun arm dropping just enough to give Cody a chance. He rushed

Vetrov, blindsiding the Russian with a tackle, knocking the weapon from his grasp.

Suddenly, Vetrov was up and whirling madly toward Cody. At the last second, he spotted the blade in Vetrov's fist and dodged. The Russian took advantage of the opening to sidle around Cody and make for the stairs.

He made it all of ten steps before Cody was on him. He hit Vetrov in the knees, but his timing was off. The Russian stumbled but remained upright. With the Devil's own luck, he reached the stairs and bolted up two at a time.

*Jackrabbit SOB,* thought Cody, surging after him. For a bearish brute of a man, the general sure could move. When Cody reached the top of the steps, Vetrov was nowhere in sight so he made for the front door.

Halfway across the dining room, he paused.

Thirty backpacks were lined up against the far wall. The cellphone in Cody's pocket was going bananas. It was obvious where the contents of the Hummingbird briefcases had ended up ...

Then he caught sight of Vetrov through the window and took off after him.

———

SARA BLASTED the two-man rocket team to bits with a burst from the Yak. Then she was soaring up, high enough to see the second wave of Furies coming across the lawn in her direction.

She peeled away, doing a 180-degree rotation before reorienting the nose to begin a strafing run. Bullets bounced off the armored body of the 24 as she dove head-first toward the line of Furies.

Then the Yak was roaring, chanting its high caliber

song of death, chugging rounds into the advancing women, reducing them to jerking marionettes of torn bone and flesh. She checked the read-out on the weapon station panel. She had just over 800 rounds left for the Yak and a half dozen air-to-ground missiles tucked under the 24's winglets.

It was time to bring this thing home.

She swung the nose of the craft toward the front of the main house.

———

VETROV WAS MAKING for a white van parked by the side of the house. Cody leapt off the porch, hit the ground running and sprinted after him. The general had eluded his grasp before. He wasn't going to let him get away this time.

That's when he saw Thelma Justice.

It was she who was behind the wheel of the van. Cody would recognize her anywhere. The distinctive face and hairstyle were obvious, even from a distance. So she was Vetrov's getaway driver...

Vetrov reached the van's side door, threw it wide and grabbed something off of the seat. Then he was spinning around, a machine-pistol in his hands. Cody dove behind a tree as a storm of bullets sliced the air where he'd been. Then a moment later the van door was slamming and the pair were peeling away.

He heard the thrum of the approaching chopper. Sara was coming in low toward the house, the 24's spotlight bathing the ground in its path. Arms waving, Cody ran into its glare.

Sara saw him, hovered and then began descending. She brough the chopper within a few feet of the ground and sprang the hatch automatically. Cody was through in an instant.

"Vetrov and Thelma! They're in that van!"

Sara nodded, slipping the hatch control toggle and putting some distance between them and the ground. The house fell away beneath them.

"What about the nukes?" she asked.

"In there. Front room." Cody pointed. "Lined up along the front wall."

Sara nodded. She was flipping buttons on the weapons console. "We're pretty well armed for bear up here," she said. "Just give me a sec..."

Re-grasping the stick, she adjusted the nose downward, stabilized the chop and touched the firing button.

Two missiles streaked toward the front of the house. The resulting explosion blew the facade to powder, tumbling columns and bricks into an untidy heap and collapsing the main floor into the tunnels below. The second explosion piled the rubble even higher, bringing the east and west wings of the entryway down in a heap. She fired two more into the piled ruins, jumbling, tossing and burying the mix so high and deep that the backpacks full of warheads were unreachable without a work crew. Then she twisted the stick and set off after Vetrov.

# CHAPTER FIFTY-NINE

THE TWISTING MOUNTAIN road rolled out ahead of them as Thelma Justice steered, keeping up a brisk but safe pace. Vetrov, in the passenger seat, kept an eye on the rear-view mirror.

"No sign of anyone," he said.

"That helicopter will be along any second," said Thelma Justice, her voice tight.

"We have a way out," he promised. "Get us to the second tunnel after the bridge. Once we get there, we can surprise them. Now go!"

———

THE SEARCHLIGHT GUIDING THEM, Sara and Cody followed the road that zigzagged between the hills. It was devoid of traffic at this hour - just a ribbon of concrete winding through the mountains. The nest of shadows between the peaks was even deeper with night. Somewhere ahead, Vetrov and Thelma Justice were fleeing their appointed date with destiny.

"Whoever designed these roads never reckoned with aerial reconnaissance," Sara complained, steering around a looming crag to keep the spotlight on the road.

"I'm doubting they'll run into any speed traps," Cody admitted. Mountainous sections of Europe were notorious for no speed limits and non-existent traffic enforcement. "On the other hand, who else would be out here at this hour?"

Sara adjusted the altitude and brought them up a hundred feet. And saw them.

"There!" She pointed at two glimmering points of red in the darkness ahead that were briefly visible before winking out behind a peak. "Got a fix on them now!"

"The nukes are secure. For now. And the jury's out." Cody narrowed his eyes. "Let's go deliver appropriate sentencing."

Sara adjusted the spotlight forward and poured on the speed. The 24 roared, diving toward the road to close in on the tiny red taillights in the distance.

———

VETROV SAW the approaching spotlight and pointed it out.

"Tunnel up ahead!" Thelma cried. Their headlights gleamed in the reflective decals surrounding the tunnel mouth.

"Drive in two hundred yards, park and kill lights," Vetrov instructed. He put his hand to the door. "Let me out here first."

She did as he instructed. Vetrov leapt from the van and stood by the mouth of the tunnel, pistol in hand.

———

THE 24 SPED ALONG, now just thirty feet off the ground and following the road toward the tunnel. Cody, hands on the fire control, leaned forward in his seat, waiting to pick off the vehicle below. The face of the mountain came up surprisingly fast.

"I'm going to have to climb," said Sara. "The tunnel - Wait!"

"There!" Cody's thumb tensed on the Yak's fire button. "Vetrov's standing ... outside the tunnel?" It was his last statement before hitting the trigger. Tracer rounds tore up the road. Flared in light, Vetrov loosed two shots from his weapon before taking off up the road.

"He's backtracking!" Cody snapped as Sara climbed up and away from the mountainside. She circled out, allowing the spotlight to guide them through the treacherous low peaks and outcroppings. She returned to the road a quarter mile back from the tunnel's mouth, retracing their progress with the spotlight. There was no sign of the van or Vetrov.

"He psyched us." Sara smiled sourly. "How much you want to bet they're blasting down that tunnel road right now?"

"Let's get after them!"

She maneuvered the stick, coaxing the chopper into a steep climb. The spotlight remained focused resolutely ahead. Rock, ice and scrub brush sailed by until clear skies returned and Sara could push the stick forward. They sailed bare feet above the mountain's plateau before descending toward the road again. Two red lights winked ahead.

"There!"

"Slippery," Cody muttered. He dropped his hands back to the weapons panel and began bringing the Yak online. "Bring us up behind them nice and slow."

"Will do, but I'll have to be careful." She squinted ahead into the dark. "Another mountain tunnel looming."

"All I need is a clear shot," said Cody. The Yak shifted in its turret. An infra-green image of the vehicle showed on the targeting monitor, swishing with each adjustment of the gun. The sights finally settled on the rear hatch. Cody pressed the fire switch.

A blizzard of tracers lit the night sky, the nose of the chopper bursting to life with deadly fire. The Yak churned out rounds, ripping up road, shredding rock, cement and signage before contacting the rear of Vetrov's getaway vehicle.

———

GLASS BLEW IN. The tracers punched holes in the roof. Then the chopper banked away. The mouth of the next tunnel glimmered in the headlights.

"STEP ON IT!" Vetrov cried, banging the dash. The engine groaned, screamed and suddenly they were sliding under the dark stone roof of the inter-mountain tunnel. "Okay, now slow down ..."

"Slow down?" Thelma Justice was in a lather. "Are you crazy? They could seal us in here!"

"No." He grasped her arm. "Look."

Up ahead, inset in the wall of the tunnel, was a maintenance door. She applied the brakes and they coasted to a stop beside it. The tunnel, still and quiet in the half-light, boasted no other vehicles, no traffic beside themselves. At a gesture from Vetrov, Thelma Justice switched off the ignition and got out to stand beside him before the maintenance door.

"What have we here, Greb?" she asked, her voice teasing despite the situation.

"Insurance policy." He dug a keychain from his pocket and fit a narrow silver key into the lock. "KGB create this back in 1980s. An emergency escape hatch for Soviet agents in France. Come see."

The door swung wide to reveal a narrow cement stairway. Lit by low emergency lighting, it descended into the bowels of the Earth. Far below, Thelma thought she could hear a rush of water.

They descended the steps, Vetrov leading, Thelma keeping hold of a narrow iron railing that lined one side. The climb down was exhausting. After twenty minutes, she checked her watch. When they finally reached the bottom, she noted that an hour had passed.

The stairway ended on a narrow stone platform. A boat was moored there – a modest cabin cruiser. Motion detectors activated floodlights as they approached the ship. Thelma could see it was polished, ship-shape and barely used.

"CIA have their Mediterranean fleet. So do we." Vetrov stepped onboard, then held out a hand to assist her. "Cody and his CIA girlfriend will land and look. They will find this place in a day. Maybe two. By then, we'll be long gone. This underground river comes out along the coast."

"So we're far from finished."

"Far." He smiled. "Very far."

# CHAPTER SIXTY

CODY AND SARA did find the abandoned van, and the stairway leading down to the deserted moorage on the underground river. It was obvious that Vetrov and Justice were long gone, God only knew where. So they flew the chopper back to the construction lot and abandoned it there in the pre-dawn hours before piling into Sara's car for the drive back to Jacquard's cottage.

"We'll pick up their trail." Sara sounded resigned. "They'll have to surface sooner or later."

"We'll get Aisha working on a list of Vetrov's known contacts in the Mediterranean and North Africa," he said. "I can get her access to an army intel database that's pretty good."

They parked in the driveway before the cottage and took a moment to just sit motionless and unwind. Neither one realized they were breathing heavily until they stopped and listened. Then they turned to one another and laughed.

"I thought we were done for," she said.

"Me too." He took her hand. "We came close a few times. But we came through."

"We did."

They kissed, hungry for each other in the afterglow of danger. The kiss lingered almost a full minute before they parted.

"Come on." He squeezed her hand. "Let's go say hi to Aisha."

They got out and let themselves into the cottage, only to discover Aisha was gone.

———

"NOT A TRACE OF HER." Sara shook her head and sat back from her own laptop. "Almost no public or private CCTV anywhere in this part of town. All her stuff is gone. No sign of a struggle. Our only guess is that she must have waited until we were gone to take a powder."

"But where?"

"Perhaps Achmed got her."

"Would he have bothered to take all her stuff?" Cody waved a hand over the table. "Laptop? Messenger bag? She even took her favorite box of tea from the cabinet. No, I -"

A knock came on the door. Both tensed and fell silent. Sara rose and padded to the window. Peering through the curtain, she relaxed. Then she stepped over and opened the door.

Parsons stood there, a cloth cap on his head, spectacles fogging in the damp cold. "May I come in?" he asked politely.

"Thank God." Sara stood aside to let him enter. "What are you doing here?"

"Just in town to make arrangements for Jacquard's widow." Parsons pulled off his jacket.

"Didn't know he was married," admitted Sara.

"Oh yes." Parsons took a seat at the table. "Wife. A few children. Several mistresses. He was, after all, French..."

"Aisha is gone."

Parsons hesitated, then said: "I know."

"Where is she?"

"I don't know." He held up a hand. "Allow me to explain. She called yesterday evening. We spoke for an hour. She wanted my opinion about Thelma Justice and her teachings. It was a long phone call because I don't know anything about Thelma Justice's philosophy so I was subjected to tedious recitations of her work..."

"Wait. What?" Cody leaned forward. "She called you up to read you bits of Thelma's books?"

"She did. Yes." Parsons produced a pack of Rothman's and lit one. "I told her what I thought in no uncertain terms. That Thelma Justice is a charlatan, no different from any of those mega-church pastors you see on American television. Dreadful stuff! Imagine *Mein Kampf* written by Oprah Winfrey. Oh, the tedium! But Aisha seemed to eat it up."

"Why did she want to talk about all this with you?"

"Said she had to make a decision." Parson's smiled thinly. "Remember when you were in Moscow and concerned about her running away?"

"Yes," they said in unison.

"We had a talk late one night sitting at the kitchen table in the Vicarage. She fell asleep at one point, laying her head in her arms. I took the opportunity..." He reached into a pocket and produced something resembling a pager. "To do this."

Cody took the device from Parsons' hand. It was a mobile tracking unit. Aisha's position was shown as a moving red dot on a digital map of France.

"I sewed a GPS tracker into the lining of her messenger bag." Parsons tapped the screen. "Seems to be headed to Paris. Vetrov, meanwhile, has appeared off the Libyan coast."

Cody turned to Sara. "So we split up. You go retrieve Aisha. I resume pursuit of Vetrov."

"Makes sense." She nodded. "We'll join you when we can."

"Near as we can tell, Vetrov's final destination is likely Syria. That's where Crimson Jihad has their main base." Parsons produced a cellphone. "Backchannel has a very good man in Syria. Hamid Hassan. Retired Mossad. I'll put him onto you."

"Excellent," said Cody. "We need to unravel Vetrov's and Justice's final plan. Only Aisha can help us do that. Whatever they're up to, it involves nukes and it's already in motion. We've got to shut it down . . ."

# EPILOGUE

*Northeast Syria*

WHEN RUMORS SPREAD that the one known as the Imam was coming, excitement gripped the village. Children ran from house to house to spread the news. The women left their washing and baking and broke out their best cookpots. The men trimmed their beards and cleaned their assault rifles. And the elders of the village slaughtered a goat in preparation for the feast to come.

Feasts were rare in their world. Successive wars and years of famine had reduced this corner of Syria to a blighted hellscape wherein little grew and game was scarce. The only benefits to living this far out in the *sahrā* were that troops were scarce, and the government's presence was almost nonexistent. The villagers were a proud, hearty people who would gladly suffer the privations of primitive life in exchange for a semblance of the freedom their ancestors had once enjoyed. Around the fire at night, they told stories of the days when their forebears had roamed the sands on horse and camel, raiding and stealing whatever they wanted, answering to no one. The more ambitious among them spoke of a revival of such greatness. But when such talk arose, the elders merely exchanged glances and remained silent. They knew the days of the villagers' greatness lay far in the past.

A brutal regime, an even more brutal occupation by the Russian military and finally the devastation of ISIS sweeping through their region had brought them to their current lowly state. With each year that passed, fewer children were born, less trade with other villages was transacted and more songs and legends from their past were forgotten. All that seemed to lie ahead for the good people of the village was oblivion as, one by one, they succumbed to the brutal indifference of history. All, indeed, seemed lost.

Until the Imam.

———

LIKE SALADIN'S, the Imam's name was one to strike terror into the hearts of his enemies. And the enemies of the common people – the little people – were his enemies.

The first indications of the Imam's presence came in whispers. Over tea, around the fire or in a scrap of newsprint, a name surfaced. Again and again, that name was repeated with ever greater embellishments…

> … *massacred government troops in their barracks as they slept…*
> … *fought the Russians to a standstill at the Battle of the Great Wadi…*
> … *even the Americans were forced to broker terms with him…*

Until the day he appeared in the flesh and changed the lives of the villagers forever.

His arrival was heralded by a pillar of dust that rose skyward in the distance. The young men who acted as lookouts for the village reported that a huge column of ISIS fighters was streaming this way. But when the women reacted with horror, the young men laughed. For the ISIS marauders were not massing in force to descend on the village, but rather were in a jumbled and tangled hurry to flee something.

Or some*one*.

It took hours for the soldiers of the Caliphate to file through the village, a listless rabble. It turned out that the young men had been right: rather than the hard-eyed, ruthless killers that burned and beheaded all in their path, the column that trudged through had consisted of beaten men. Broken men. Men *frightened.*

Of him.

The Imam.

———

Now ANOTHER COLUMN of dust rose in the distance. The boys acting as lookouts ran into the village square.

"He is coming! He is coming! The one sent by Allah! The Imam is at the gates!"

Expressions of joy passed among the villagers. The men puffed out their chests. The women sang. And the children played joyfully. Only the elders shared knowing glances and remained silent. They had seen too much to place faith in any earthly man.

———

ENSCONCED in the backseat of the captured Humvee Selim Farah Mohammed, also known as 'the Imam' and 'the White Wolf', anticipated his arrival in the village. To be sure, he would be pleased to see the villagers again. Simple people such as they – hard-working, devout, family-focused – were the reason he fought. He believed the corruption of *Shaitan* lay not only in the hearts of Westerners but also within the leadership of the Arab world. Impelled by the same temptations of money and easy living, such men had become compromised and the people had been forsaken. The White Wolf loved the company of the forsaken.

But it was not because of them that he was visiting the village. Not today.

The White Wolf rode in a caravan of captured military vehicles. From the Russians his men had taken tanks and Humvees. From the Syrians, armored personnel carriers. And from ISIS, a motley collection of pick-up trucks and troop transport vehicles. Mismatched in shape and color, they nevertheless proceeded in step, crisply spaced, their synchronization flawless. Above each one flew the scarlet banner of the movement the White Wolf had founded.

Crimson Jihad.

The column slowed as it approached the village. The simple villagers thronged the one dirt street that ran through the center of their community. The White Wolf leaned forward and waved to them through the window, his heart gladdened by their smiling faces and voices uplifted in chanting their name for him: *Imam*. Literally, one learned in the Holy Q'uran.

The White Wolf knew the Q'uran better than some clerics. Once, his mother had held out hope he might study the Mother of All Books and become leader of his own mosque. But his studies had taught him that the Word of Allah was not for preaching, but for setting fire to the civilizations of the infidels.

At length, his vehicle stopped before the house of the village headman. Although the largest dwelling in town, it was still modest by any standard. The headman himself appeared at the doorway to greet him.

"*Salaam,* Imam. You honor our humble village with your presence."

"*Salaam* to you, my friend." The White Wolf stepped forward and embraced his host. "Are the others here?"

"No, great one. You are the first to arrive."

The village elder led the White Wolf into the front room. Per custom, he offered his guest a bowl and a pitcher of fresh water to wash his hands and feet. The White Wolf thanked the man and dipped in gratefully. Not for him some ceremonial sprinkling of water on the fingertips: he embraced village ways, ancient ways right down to his core. He washed, dried himself with the plain cloth towels provided and went to the door.

The villagers had gathered in the town square and were pointing skyward. Their voices rose in an excited hubbub at the approaching helicopter. Such wonders accompanied the Imam! But their excitement grew to puzzlement and then fear when they recognized the Russian insignia on the vehicle's tail. The great beast chopped and snapped at the air with its twin rotors, circling above the village before coming to rest in a nearby field. The doors rolled open and two men emerged.

That they were foreigners was obvious to anyone observing their pale white skin and fair hair. That they were Russian soldiers was immediately obvious to every member of the village, each one of whom had personal experience of pain and suffering inflicted at the hands of these invaders, the supposed "allies" of their president – a man most wouldn't bother to piss on if he was on fire.

The White Wolf stepped out and greeted the senior of the two men with a handclasp.

"Colonel. So good to see you."

"Hello, sir. General Vetrov sends his regards."

"And the soldiers and martyrs of Crimson Jihad salute the great general. Please convey to him my deepest compliments."

"I will do that, sir." The Colonel turned and spoke to his assistant briefly in Russian, dispatching the man to wait back at the chopper. Then the Colonel and the White Wolf entered the headman's home.

"The general asked me to convey his apologies for not coming personally." The Colonel doffed his boots at the door per custom and took a seat on a thick floor cushion. "He has been occupied in France. Unfortunately, our activities there have come to the attention of the American CIA. He has been occupied with settling those affairs."

"Of course. But we are still agreed on the terms of our arrangement, yes?"

"Definitely, yes. Circumstances dictate some changes be made but our deal stands."

"Good."

A vehicle pulled up to the front of the headman's house, delivering the third and final attendee of today's meeting. The vehicle, a Range Rover, was driven by a local tour guide. Two men with AKs sat in the back seat. The two other passengers were women. The one in back, attired in a military uniform, stepped out and opened the door for the passenger in the front seat, coming to attention when she stepped to the ground.

Windy Duke, personal assistant to Thelma Justice, entered the house and received the headman's welcome. Once she had doffed her shoes and washed, she took a seat on a pillow across from the Colonel and the White Wolf.

"Sorry to keep you waiting." She flashed a brilliant smile. "Ms. Justice and General Vetrov thought this meeting would be a good idea."

"Yes." The Colonel turned to the White Wolf. "We have encountered a slight delay in securing the items we promised to deliver. This is entirely natural and par for the course given the sort of operation involved. To avoid risk of discovery, we are covering our tracks. And this change of plan has afforded us an opportunity we might not otherwise have considered."

"We have gained access to something even better than the Hummingbirds. We have the opportunity to seize the Sword of Damocles. And wield it against our common enemy."

"You plan to turn America's weapons back on itself?"

"With your help, yes." The Colonel sat forward anxiously. "Our intent is to coordinate operations with your organization. So there will be two components. One will involve disruptions in some major western cities by ground forces. That is how we hope Crimson Jihad can help us."

"And the other component?"

Windy smiled. "It will come… from on high."

"We have gained a great deal of knowledge about the cyber security protocols of the American aerospace defense forces," explained the Colonel. "It is our intent to hijack American aerospace assets and turn them against their creators."

"Our common enemy," said the White Wolf. His

heart began to beat faster as he imagined the joy his men would experience murdering infidels.

"If we join our forces, we will bring ruin down upon all who oppose us," said Windy Duke.

"Let us celebrate our new venture with a glass of tea," suggested the Colonel.

"Praise Allah," said the White Wolf.

## A LOOK AT BOOK THREE:
### FINAL STRIKE

**Time Has Run Out!**

The fuse can't burn any shorter. An insane media megastar, Thelma Justice, and her power-hungry lover, a Russian nuclear arms dealer, are close to unleashing hell on earth.

CIA field agents Jack Cody and Sara Durrell have gone rogue. On the run, operating without official sanction, they're the only two people on earth with any chance of preventing a mad scheme of imminent global destruction. But now their own country is after them!

With a young, hot-blooded Dubai princess to deal with and with more than one hit team closing in from every side, Sara and the man they call Suicide Cody must try to stay alive as they track a twisting trail of deceit and sudden death from the blood-soaked desert sands of Syria to the icy killing fields high atop the rugged Italian Alps in a race against time to prevent the ultimate doomsday scenario.

*"Stephen Mertz is the best action writer I've read in a long time . . . the Cody's War series is filled with everything you want from a master writer!"* —Brent Towns, bestselling author of the *Team Reaper* series.

### *AVAILABLE APRIL 2022*

# ABOUT THE AUTHOR

**Stephen Mertz** is an American fiction author who is best known for his mainstream thrillers and novels of suspense. His work covers a wide variety of styles from paranormal dark suspense (*Night Wind* and *Devil Creek*) to historical speculative thrillers (*Blood Red Sun*) and hardboiled noir (*Fade to Tomorrow*). Mertz is also a popular lecturer on the craft of writing and has appeared as a guest speaker before writer's groups and at universities.

During high school and college, Steve regularly scandalized his "literary, well-intentioned" creative writing teachers with "thud and blunder melodramas." Throughout military service, travel, and a wide variety of jobs, his goal remained to become a publishing, full-time freelance professional. "It was never a question for me of if, but always when." His first national sale was to a mystery magazine, and his first novel, a detective thriller entitled *Some Die Hard*, was published under the pseudonym of Stephen Brett. Another Brett novel followed, as did a string of mystery and suspense short stories.

Steve's writing output increased dramatically when he emerged as one of the country's most in-demand writers of adventure paperback novels, averaging four books per year for ten years. His work on Don Pendleton's Mack Bolan series is regarded by fans as some of the best in that series. He also created the Mark Stone:

MIA Hunter and Cody's Army series, written under the pseudonyms Jack Buchanan and Jim Case respectively.

Stephen Mertz has traveled widely and is a U.S. Army veteran. He presently lives in the American Southwest, and he is always at work on a new book.